MW01128894

This book is a work of fiction. The names, characters, places, and incidents are products of the writer's imagination or have been used fictitiously and are not to be construed as real. Any resemblance to persons, living or dead, actual events, locale or organizations is entirely coincidental.

Ben Knight has held a lot of titles—devoted son, big brother to six siblings, captain of the Marine's Fleet Anti-Terrorism Security Team and his best-known gig of Louisiana playboy. But the ladies are just going to have to understand that his time's stretched thin when he takes on the leadership of a new special ops force.

With his brothers as sidekicks.

Worst idea ever. But a decision Ben has no control over, and control is his middle name. Actually, it's Bartholomew but thank God nobody knows that, except one pretty little brown-eyed Cajun girl with access to too much information about the Knight family and an oh-so-sweet sassy mouth. A mouth that he's never forgotten even though it's been three months since he's last had her in his bed, against a wall and over a barstool.

Dahlia was a victim of the notorious Ben Knight's love-'em-and-leave-'em lifestyle, and it ticks her off that she can't forget him. Maybe it's that bad-boy smile or the way he looks like sin poured into low-slung jeans. When he comes sniffing around again, her libido makes her jump into action—and straight into a world of secrets surrounding Ben. Leading her to question whether her heart can withstand a life with a man who might not be alive tomorrow.

All Knighter

by

Em Petrova

Chapter One

This was the fuckin' life. Ass on barstool, drink in hand, looking between a pretty waitress flitting back and forth behind the bar and the Astros game on the flat-screen.

Ben Knight wasn't wearing eighty pounds of gear while hiking through combat zones or even sporting a wristwatch since he didn't give a damn about the time, but he was packing heat. He didn't go anywhere without his M-9 Beretta, though he'd spent enough time overseas that he'd become very fond of foreign sidearms.

As he lifted his drink to his lips again, a cheer went up around the bar. Unaware why the patrons of the New Orleans hole-in-the-wall were making a ruckus, Ben looked at the TV to see the hitter running the bases, but a glance back at the cute blonde showed that her denim miniskirt had ridden up her tanned thighs. He cocked a smile. It had been pretty high to begin with.

Could be cheering at either one. Right now, his bets were on the girl.

Ben was a master of concealment, so when the bartender caught him staring at her ass, it was entirely purposeful.

With a coy look, she sauntered up to face him across the wooden bar top and leaned in so he could also see down her shirt. Both the top and bottom halves of this woman's body seemed to match—all curves and sultry Southern nights.

"So, Cowboy," she said with a twinkle in her eyes, "are you who I think you are?"

"I am if you've got the time."

"Hey, quit hogging the bartender! Jennifer, I could use a drink," a patron called from the opposite end of the bar.

Jennifer gave Ben a smile and a wink before twitching her curves to the other end of the bar.

He tugged on the brim of his Stetson and paused. The action shouldn't cause all the hair on his nape to stand on end. Which could only mean one thing-- danger.

He slid his hand along his side, inches from the weapon tucked in his waistband.

"Don't move for your weapon, Captain." The words came low, but Ben had the hearing of a fucking German Shepard and everything in him was on red alert.

Ben didn't bother turning his head right or left where the two men bracketed him on his stool. He wrapped his fingers around his glass again. "If you boys're calling me captain, then you must be Marines. Join me for a drink?"

"Your presence is required by Colonel Jackson, sir."

He took a bracing swallow of the whiskey and pushed out a sigh. "I'm not only off-duty, gentlemen, but I'm retired."

The man on his left gripped his biceps and the other gripped his right. "We have orders to drag you off this stool and put you in the trunk of our vehicle if you don't comply, Captain."

"Jesus Christ." Was this really happening? All Ben wanted was peace and quiet, but his error had been in postponing his trip to the Keys. He shouldn't have made a pitstop in Louisiana to visit his family and gone straight for the golf and the sunshine.

He shook his head. "I suppose Colonel Jackson's outside in said vehicle, am I right?"

"No, sir. He's here in New Orleans."

"Well," he knocked back the rest of his whiskey and set the glass on the bar, "I guess that means I'm going with you. Mind letting go of my arms so I can pay for my drink?"

Around them, the bar was erupting with cheers again, and this time he knew it was for the Astros, who'd just cleaned the bases. The pretty blonde had moved on to another man and was displaying her wares to him.

Ben sighed. It might have been fun. Some playtimes weren't—many were. For five years, he'd been with FAST—the special ops team that guarded

3

sensitive naval installations, including ones involving nukes. But Ben had another acronym for FAST.

Fucking All Sexy Turn-ons.

That was his new mission, and about the only thing he was devoted to at the moment, besides whiskey, golf and sunshine. Apparently, he was putting those vices aside for the moment and visiting with Colonel Jackson.

The men released his arms and Ben reached for his wallet. For a split second, he considered going for his weapon, but what good would it do to be retired and on the run?

He tossed a few bills on the bar and got up. The air conditioning in the shitty bar couldn't keep up with the Louisiana heat, and his jeans felt sticky, his thin cotton T-shirt clinging to his lower back.

Finally, he faced the men who'd been sent to collect him. He snorted. "Christ, you guys get younger and younger."

"Yes, sir," one agreed.

Shaking his head, Ben gestured to the door. "Shall we? If you don't mind, I'd prefer to drive rather than riding in the trunk."

Ten minutes later, Ben screeched to a stop in front of the facility that was really a small group of buildings that pencil-pushers liked to call a base, when really high-ranking officers just used it as a place to take a piss when passing through.

4

Ben cut the engine and threw a look at the guy in the passenger's seat and then the one in the back. Both had been white-knuckling it as he took the well-known Louisiana roads like a Nascar driver.

He threw them a grin. "Thanks for the ride, boys."

He got out and walked in like he owned the place.

Colonel Jackson's bellow sounded the instant the door closed. "Is that Ben Knight? Get his ass in here. Now."

Two second-lieutenants came out of nowhere to flank Ben.

"By all means, show me the way," he joked.

They didn't smile. No, they were busy being good Marines and kissing ass. Colonel Jackson's ass, to be exact. Those days were over for Ben. He'd put in his time. The only thing on his mind from here on out was a rod and reel, a bag of golf clubs and a nonstop stream of beautiful women in his bed.

He was led into a room with a gleaming smoky glass table and a dozen empty chairs circling it.

Ben released a whistle. "Rather a large reception for me, but I don't mind some hoopla."

Colonel Jackson whipped from the window and set his glare on Ben. "Damn, you're just as reckless as you were back in North Korea. What took you so long to get here, might I ask? By my calculations, the journey from the… what was it? The Voodoo Bar should have taken no more than twelve minutes."

"Ten, with my driving sir."

Jackson pulled back his uniform cuff and checked his watch. Then he arched his brows at Ben.

"I had to finish my whiskey first, Colonel."

"Dammit, Knight. Stand at attention. And take off that goddamn cowboy hat." He pointed to a spot in front of him. Ben's reflexes kicked in and he snapped straight upright, heels together and salute ready, Stetson on the table. He felt the officer's gaze moving over him, probably assessing the sweat stains he bore, his too-long hair and the scruff of beard he'd refused to shave since retiring.

"At ease, captain." He circled him and sniffed. "Whiskey… Do I need to give you a sobriety test, Knight, or are you sober enough to hear what I have to say?"

"Meaning no disrespect, sir, but I didn't have enough drinks to even give me a buzz, sir."

"Enough of your mouth. Take a seat."

As Ben pulled out a chair and sat, the two guys who'd flanked him moved to the door and placed their backs to either side, guarding it. From what? Ben couldn't help but feel he was being barricaded inside, but what the hell for? He was done, had the official papers to prove it. No more bullets flying by his head, just sun on water and drinks served up by women scantily clad in bikinis.

Jackson took a chair at the head of the table and steepled his fingers, his gray eyes piercing over the tips. Ben had survived more stressful experiences than being stared at by a commanding officer, so he rested his arms on the table and waited.

"You're a cocky asshole, you know it, Knight?"

"I've been told that, sir."

"You started out at Lejeune, moved up quickly to first lieutenant. Deployed to Afghanistan in '13. Then quickly became one of the FAST team, where you did some good in North Korea."

Ben swung his gaze to the colonel. "All due respect, sir, but we did more than some 'good' in North Korea."

"Don't get mouthy with me, Captain. I know exactly what you did there. But that's classified, isn't it?" The way he drawled told Ben this man was a native of Louisiana, the accent too close to his own native roots, no matter how many years either of them had spent outside the state.

The drawl also reminded him—vividly—of a dark-haired, sloe-eyed *belle femme* he'd spent a weekend holed up with after being in North Korea. The things that woman could do with her mouth…

Well, now wasn't the place to consider that, was it?

Jackson eyed him. Ben eyed him back.

"Damn, but you're a snot-nosed brat of a Marine, aren't you, Knight?" He sat back in his seat. "If I

7

didn't need your skills right now, I'd kick you out of my office for stinking like whiskey."

So, they were getting to the crux of his visit at last.

"Permission to ask what you need me for, Colonel. I might remind you I'm retired."

"You don't need to remind me of jack shit, Knight. What I have for you is a team."

Ben nearly groaned and felt his dreams of golfing in the Keys and drinking rum all day washing out from under him like sand in the Gulf.

Jackson narrowed one eye at him. "Ever hear of Operation Freedom Flag?"

Dammit, Ben knew he wouldn't be allowed to kick back and relax for the rest of his days. They were going to ask him to serve his country further and using his own fucking patriotism to manipulate him into doing it. It was damn easy to bury his head in the sand and ignore the world events that he'd been so embroiled in for years. But Operation Freedom Flag was a brand-new team created on American soil to protect in ways Homeland failed to. Bigger, deeper, scarier shit.

"I can see you know it," Jackson went on. "We need a team, special ops like FAST, but more centralized to the South. Lots of bad shit goin' on down here, Knight."

He pushed out a sigh. "Not surprising, Colonel."

"Don't be insolent with me. Now we need you, Knight. When General Heyr sat down with me, the commander of ICE and even the goddamn Vice President of the United States, your name was the one that continued to come up. In fact, the *only* one to come up."

Fuck, this was worse than he'd imagined. He wished to hell he was still back on that barstool ogling the blonde's ass. Or better yet, off to the oldest section of New Orleans to locate the dark beauty that had stirred his blood so right all those months ago.

"You would be heading Operation Freedom Flag Southern US division, Knight."

"Heading? How many men are we talking about?"

"OFFSUS would have the best of the best, I assure you, Knight."

He rolled with the acronym, already identifying with it and seating himself in charge. Dammit to hell, all he wanted was to hit eighteen holes.

"If I take this, Colonel, do I get to choose my men?" He already had a few in mind—guys he'd served with, brothers who'd—

"I've already done that for you, Knight." Jackson looked over his head and nodded to the guards. Seconds later, through the window on the far wall, Ben could see the vehicles pouring onto the property.

An El Camino painted in Tuxedo Black. Only one man could drive such a pimped out Southern car.

Ben didn't even get a chance to open his mouth to speak when the second vehicle had his molars grinding. The Jeep with the top down left no question as to who was behind the wheel — cocky sunglasses and all.

The practical economy car in third place could be anyone, though. It *had* to be anyone. Please let it be anyone else, Ben thought.

But the Ninja motorcycle rolling in last left no doubt.

He swallowed the anger and acid of the words he was about to spew at a commanding officer. "What the hell is this, Colonel?" was enough to earn him a sharp look.

"I take it you recognize your new team, Knight."

"Team?"

The doors opened and Ben whirled to glare at the Marines striding in, each as big and full of themselves as he was. Nobody but a Knight could be.

"Jesus Christ," he muttered. "My brothers are the men I'm to command?"

"Hey, Ben. I see you've gotten some sun," Sean threw out as he circled the table and plopped into the seat opposite him.

"You little shit ass — "

A clap on his back had him turning to lock gazes with Chaz, the blonder of the five Knight brothers, though everyone teased him that his hair just bleached out with the top of his Jeep down in the baking Louisiana sun.

Chaz shoved his glasses up on his head and offered a crooked grin. "Good to see ya again, bro."

Ben had just eaten a Sunday meal with his family and nobody had uttered a word about this new special ops team—or that they were part of it. Had they known? He didn't think Dylan was capable of hiding anything, so he turned to him as he entered the room.

He took a double-take. "What's with the nerd glasses, Dylan?"

His little brother sported horn-rimmed glasses, which were new.

Dylan gave him a crooked smile and waggled his brows above the frames. "Givin' them a test run."

"You can't be on my team with poor vision. Colonel—" He spun to look at Jackson, who was smiling at him. Too late, Ben realized what he'd said.

His team. Goddammit.

"My eyesight's just as perfect as it was back when I was in sniper training, Ben. Don't get your boxers in a twist. These glasses have other features."

Ben could only imagine the gadgets Dylan loved toying with. Not only was he a master of weapons and a sniper with a near-perfect record of accuracy, but he was brilliant with technology. He'd hacked the damn Pentagon at seventeen, which had earned him a ride straight to the nearest prison cell—and then he'd

11

been recruited directly to the US government. Dylan hadn't even finished high school before he'd been set up hacking electronics and decoding correspondence. Then he'd claimed to have "gotten bored" and enlisted in the Marines like his brothers, where he'd become a top sniper.

And Rhoades... Dammit, Ben's youngest brother was hardly out of boot camp. Could barely wipe his own ass. Now he was riding a crotch rocket and was the final man entering the room.

The Knight boys all took seats and stared at Ben, along with Jackson, the sneaky bastard.

"You knew this," Ben accused, wagging a finger at his family members.

They started shaking their heads, when Jackson said, "I just notified them earlier today, Captain. Now sit."

Directly disobeying an order, he looked back to the door. "We need six on a team. Should I expect Tyler to walk through that door next?" It wouldn't surprise him one fucking bit to see their little sister, one of the twins, enter with her sassy attitude.

He groaned.

"You'll be getting that sixth man, rest assured, Captain. Now sit and let's lay this out on the table."

Ben stiffly sat and glared at each and every one of his brothers. Stupid fuckers, all of them. The Knights were a military family, but that didn't mean they needed to be dumb, and he was seriously questioning their brain capacities right now.

"You realize if something happens to any one of us, our parents have lost a son. Right?" He directed his question at the room.

Sean lifted a shoulder and let it drop. "Nothing new there, Ben, whether we're fighting with you or another captain. Calm down."

"If I'm your captain, then what I say goes." He pointed at each. "And you, you, you and you can all go. I'm not fucking leading my brothers on missions that could get one of them — or all of us — killed." He glared now at Jackson and didn't even give a damn if he was court martialed and shot against a wall.

Chaz spread his hands. As he moved, his mirrored glasses on his head caught the light from above and reflected. "Ben, we're here to stay. We're not kids and you can't boss us around."

"Except as your fucking captain, I fucking can."

"But you cannot let go of the men I've hand-selected for OFFSUS, Knight. So get over thinking that. You've got the best of the best sitting right here, able to handle any threat you come up against, domestic or foreign."

"Jesus," he muttered. Boiling inside, he considered what Jackson was saying. His brothers had all the guts, glory and stupid Knight genetics to handle anything. Hell, they were the best shots — Ben had seen them in action and given them pointers himself. They had all the capabilities to be one of the top special operatives team in the world.

"Hell."

"*Maman* would wash your mouth out with soap," Rhoades drawled.

Their mother had no place in this conversation. Ben narrowed his eyes at him and then turned to Jackson. "Who's our six?"

"Rockingham. Seal Team 4."

"A squid?"

"A highly-trained professional who's proven himself in unspeakable situations. And the perfect man for OFFSUS, Knight."

All five of the brothers stared at the colonel at the use of their names. Ben resisted running a hand over his face and hoping it woke him from whatever fucking nightmare he was living through right now.

Because he didn't want to live through the reality of training these idiots he called family as the men who'd have his back—and each other's. Suddenly, the weight of that duty fell like a yoke over his shoulders.

How was he going to keep them all safe for his *maman* and *pére* while combating terrorism on US soil?

He dropped against the back of his chair and stared up at the ceiling. "All I wanted to do was fish, golf and fuck."

Jackson got up and slapped him on the shoulder on his way out of the room. "You'll find a way to do those things and still save the country, Captain."

* * * * *

"9-1-1, what's your call?"

"I have to cancel a date with a friend and she's not going to be very happy with me."

Dahlia glanced at her coworkers, hoping to hell her supervisor didn't overhear this personal call.

Into her mouthpiece, she hissed, "Serena, you know you can't call here!"

"Well, you weren't answering your cell and I didn't know how to reach you to break our plans for drinks."

Dahlia pushed out a sigh. This was the third time with Serena and the second this week alone one of her girlfriends had cancelled plans with her, and it was only Wednesday. It looked like her social life was well and truly over since every single one of her group of friends was now married. Dahlia had just dropped her last bridesmaid dress into Goodwill, thankful the bridezillas would calm down and they could have fun again. Or talk about something besides menus and seating plans.

Now it didn't look as if they'd ever talk at all.

"All right, that's fine. I'll take a raincheck." Dahlia stared at her fingernails. Maybe she could get another manicure tonight, but her nails didn't really need pampering. She needed some one-on-one time, talking to a human who wasn't in distress on the phone line.

She wanted to whine to Serena that her job was high-stress and she couldn't just go home and plop in front of the TV to unwind. She needed some way to de-stress, and that had always been with the help of her friends.

"I'm really sorry, Dahlia. But Mike wants to catch that new movie and since it's matinee price night and dollar Cokes, we can save some cash. You know we're saving for a down-payment for a house."

She pinched the bridge of her nose. "Yes, yes." She had to get her friend off the line in case someone really needed her. "I'll text later. Bye!"

She hurriedly disconnected the call and glanced around again. Her supervisor was not walking between operators per usual.

He was standing beside her desk. "What were you helping that woman with, Dahlia? The decision about the Coke she's getting at the movies?"

Dahlia gulped. "I'm really sorry about that, Kyle. I've told my friends never to call here."

He stared down at her until she squirmed. He was a hard-ass on the best of days, but it *was* people's lives they were dealing with. Somebody had to keep them from screwing off.

Dahlia reached under her desk into her big bag that held her knitting. She fucking hated knitting, but it was a pastime most of the operators, even the male ones, took up because they could drop it fast when a call came in. A mindless task they could switch gears from in a blink. And in this business, a blink could mean a life.

She set the needles at angles and took off on her knit and purl. The soft cream-colored wool slid through her fingers. With a final glower, Kyle moved off and she breathed a sigh of relief.

Though she was still upset at Serena dropping their girl-date, what could she do about it? The only answer was to find a new group of friends. She glanced at her coworkers. One was retired military, happily married. And Joanie had been sitting in that chair since before Moses was written into the Bible, Dahlia was sure of it.

No—drinks with coworkers was out of the question. She'd just have to go home and sit there trying not to think of the two-car accident or fire calls she'd already received tonight. Or the hysterical caller Dahlia had walked through delivering CPR to her aging dad. This call had ended well—she'd gotten the man breathing before the ambulance had arrived. But so many didn't end well.

Which was why Dahlia needed her down-time.

She clacked her needles together so hard that Joanie looked up from her own knitting. "Everything okay, Dahlia?"

She nodded and bit her lip. If she went out tonight, where would she go? A club where she could sit at a bar and blend in, maybe talk to a few people next to her. Or dance.

At the thought of getting on a crowded dance floor, a shiver ran through her, warm and slippery. God, the dance floor... last time she'd gone clubbing alone, she'd landed in the arms—and bed—of a man who'd rocked her world.

She could nearly feel those big, callused hands sliding down her bare arms, knuckles boldly skimming the outer curves of her breasts and his stare pinning her in place. "What do you say we get outta here?" His drawl had been all Louisiana, his pillow-talk the stuff of erotic stories and what was between his legs—

Her earpiece buzzed. She dropped her knitting into the bag and took the call.

"9-1-1, what's your call?"

"I-I wrecked my parents' car. I-I..."

"All right, calm down. I'm here with you. Can you tell me your name?"

"Alexis."

"Okay, Alexis, I'm Dahlia. I'm right here with you. Are you injured? Did you hit your head?"

"I don't know. I think so. The airbag blew up and my nose hurts."

"Okay, are you still in the car? Or did you get out?"

"I-I'm standing beside the road."

"Does your car look all right? Not smoking or on fire?"

"No, but it's wrecked so bad. My mom's gonna kill me!" Wails sounded for several seconds before Dahlia got the poor teen calmed down and to a safe place along the road where she wouldn't get hit by oncoming vehicles.

"I've got the paramedics on the way as well as the police, who will assist you with getting the car to safety."

"The police! Oh, man, this is really bad."

"No, it's not bad, Alexis. These people are here to help you and your mother will just be happy that you're safe. Stay on the line with me until help arrives."

She spoke to her for several more minutes, discussing after-school activities the girl was involved in like volleyball and that she had a job dog-walking during weekdays and babysitting on weekends. When she ended the call, Dahlia blew out a breath.

She could probably do this job a whole lot better if she wasn't such an empath. Each caller she listened to, Dahlia identified with, *felt* for. She couldn't put those feelings aside easily.

But she had with Ben, the hot guy who'd taken her home that night months ago. Everything about that man, from the way he danced to the flip of his tongue against hers had ignited her.

19

After a night like never before, she'd woken to find nothing more than a note, scribbled on the back of a piece of junk mail, thanking her for the night. No phone number, no let's hook up for drinks.

She'd never returned to the club again, for fear she'd see him leaving with some other victim of his sex appeal. But maybe it was time to go back. If she'd found one gem in the crowd, she could again, and this one might be worth more than a one-night stand.

She glanced at her watch. Two hours before her shift ended, and then she'd slip down to the club and look for another Ben.

Chapter Two

"Jesus Christ," Sean said for the third time.

"You haven't done anything but take the Lord's name in vain since we left that place," Dylan said from the back seat.

Ben kept his eyes glued to the road leading out of Mississippi, but he wasn't seeing the landscape. His mind was back on that compound he and his brothers had just raided, just like Sean's was.

He threw his kid brother a look. It was bad enough he felt responsible for the well-being—and that included mental health—of his team, but he didn't want to fuck up his brother for life. And the shit they'd just seen and done was the stuff of nightmares.

"Can we stop for food?" Chaz asked.

Ben glanced in the rearview mirror at the wall of flesh taking up every corner of the SUV. At least the colonel had given them a vehicle big enough for all of the Knights to fit in, which was no small feat. They were all huge, except the youngest, Rhoades, who wasn't even a fucking man. Though he was rivaling even Ben for height, leaving him thinking Rhoades just may be the biggest Knight by the time he filled out in the shoulders.

"Guys, I gotta take a piss. This ride's smooth, but the shocks aren't that great way back here," Chaz said.

"This is just like a fucking family road trip," Ben grumbled. "Where would you like me to stop? We're in butt-fuck M'ss'ssippi." Slurring the word, he waved at the windshield, which was nothing but road and scrubby trees on either side.

"I can take a leak anywhere, but I'm willin' to wait on the food." Chaz's teeth flashed white through the fading evening light filtering through the tinted windows.

"Fine, I'll stop. Any of you other motherfuckers have to take a piss, now's your time, because I'm not stopping again until I get out of this godforsaken state." Ben veered off the highway near a cluster of trees and threw the SUV into park. As his brothers climbed out and lined up along the road to take a whiz, Ben and Sean remained.

"That was fucking insane back there," Sean said quietly.

"No shit."

"Did you know what we were walking into?"

"Hell no. I knew the same as you—that we were raiding a compound with some *couyon* homegrown terrorist who had too much explosive on site and a lot of people following his gospel."

22

Sean nodded at the reference to the guy being crazy as Chaz bounced into the back seat again. "What are we talkin' about?"

Neither answered.

"Now c'mon, guys. No secrets in Knight Ops." How the hell Chaz managed to smile after seeing what they had and doing what they'd done, Ben had no fucking clue. He must be a better Marine than him.

But he straightened at what he'd said. "Knight Ops?"

"Yeah, fits, don't ya think?"

The rest of the brothers piled in. Ben got on the road.

This wasn't the first time he'd led men to do unspeakable acts, and following those moments, he'd debriefed each one, letting them tell their side of the story. There was a healing in the speaking of things.

"All right, guys, I need to know everything you did, said and thought. Starting with Chaz."

Silence descended.

"You want us to tell you what happened back there, Ben? I'm pretty sure it was you picking up those dead bodies too," Rhoades said.

He shook himself. "Yeah, I remember and likely will for a long time. Which is why we're discussing it. Then we're going to cross the Louisiana border, get us some grits and crawfish. After that, we're going to find a way to decompress. I don't give a shit if you

23

find a hooker. Just get this out of your system, starting now."

His tone laid down the law, and Chaz started talking. Each of them added on to the story, one by one, until it all came out. Crazy homegrown terrorist with two hundred followers locked in his compound, "testing" his new street drug and listening to his word about the world being against them. Chaz and Dylan had taken the back door and located enough explosives to wipe the small town off the Mississippi map and leave a crater the size of the Grand Canyon.

Then Ben and the rest had stormed the front and walked in on what seemed at first to be a party. Except all the guests were twitching like zombies, jaws slack and eyes vacant. Within seconds of entering the compound, the crazy leader had stepped out with an automatic and explosives strapped to him like a vest.

Ben and his brothers had taken the man and disarmed the bomb he wore in seconds, but the dancers kept dancing, oblivious to their surroundings. Until they all fell down and croaked, that was.

He swiped a hand over his face, unable to stop seeing the unnatural movements of those people even in the throes of death.

Suddenly, he knew how he was going to unwind. The only way to erase the memory was to see people dance to *real* music and not whatever they heard in their heads after taking a shitload of poison.

And maybe find a woman or five to fuck. Yeah, an orgy sounded real good right about now. After those grits, of course.

Telling their story had the exact effect Ben had hoped for. The guys were laughing and joking. Dylan had ripped a fart and they were all diving for their windows to get fresh air.

Sean was even sporting a crooked grin. "You're right, Ben. It's just like a family road trip. *Maman* would be proud."

"I'm sure," Ben said dryly as they stuck their heads out their windows again. Dylan sat there grinning at his accomplishment, all of them much lighter than they'd been ten minutes before.

"Look at all Rocko missed. When is our sixth man joining us anyway?" Roades asked about Rockingham.

Ben glanced in the rearview mirror at him. "Soon. He was delayed getting out of the country."

Sean twisted in his seat. "So what's the plan, guys? The cabin's not far over the state line. I say we stop for supplies and hole up there for a few days. Fish, catch some gators. Drink beer."

"You guys can. But I'm going back to New Orleans," Ben drawled, not taking his gaze off the highway.

"What's in New Orleans? You got some pussy?"

"A lot of pussy in New Orleans for the Knights," Ben said, his own lips quirking slightly at one corner.

"But no. Just gotta see something. I'll drop you guys off and take that old motorcycle in, leave you the Knight bus to get back home."

They all laughed at his referral to the vehicle. When they passed the sign for the state line, a cheer went up, and Ben pulled into the first roadside food joint he saw.

They drew a lot of stares as they packed away enough rations for a whole platoon of Marines and then piled back into the SUV and headed to the cabin. The sight and smell of the swamp conjured good feelings of homecoming, and Ben was feeling slightly lighter by the time he dropped off his brothers and kickstarted the old bike.

He took the roads at top speed, leaning hard into the curves, letting the cool air wash over his face and hoping it erased more of the crap collected in his brain after the day's events.

Somehow, his thoughts revolved back to Dahlia. The woman had gotten in his blood after just one night, and he wanted a second night just to see if he was entertaining a fantasy rather than reality. She couldn't be *that* good.

His mind wandered all over those curves. Ripe breasts and hips a man could grab onto, ankles that had made a good starting point for kissing and movie-star plump lips to end at. Everything between was *délicieux*.

By the time he rolled into the parking lot of the club, his cock was already hard. He swung his leg over the bike and crossed the gravel to the door, the bass of the music greeting him. It was only Wednesday, but Cajuns knew how to get their party on. They'd invented the *fais do-do*.

He paused with his fingers on the handle, the bass vibrating into his hand. All of a sudden, he wasn't sure if seeing people dancing was what he needed, after all. After that brisk drive home, he was feeling half-human again. He didn't need to blur the lines between what he'd seen with the zombie dancers back in the compound and the real-life ones here in the club where he'd found Dahlia months ago.

Dahlia.

He yanked open the door and stepped into the packed house. People bumped into him from every side as he strode straight to the bar, not looking around. He needed to wrap his fingers around a glass of whiskey — fast.

When he reached the bar, the bartender lifted his jaw in greeting. "What can I get ya?"

"Dewars."

The guy dropped him a wink and grabbed the bottle and a glass.

Ben didn't know what to think about the wink, but right now all he wanted was the slow burn of alcohol sliding down his gullet.

He knocked back the whiskey and asked for another. This request didn't earn him another wink, but he wasn't looking for friendship. Cradling the glass, he turned to face the room.

For a second, he feared staring at the dancers on the crowded floor would conjure visions of the zombie dancers falling over and convulsing as the poison claimed them. But to his immeasurable relief, he only saw happy people getting their party on.

The alcohol was working its way into his system and he felt the tense pull of the muscles in his shoulders begin to relax. The Cajun hillbilly music had some odd techno infusion, but Ben didn't give a damn what was playing, as long as it wasn't silent.

He stood at the side of the floor, watching pretty girls moving with their pretty friends, sparkly tops reflecting the lights. Couples bobbed to the beat, standing close with their heads together, talking over the music.

Ben was happy to be off the job and away from his brothers, who'd surely be setting up poles for night fishing and cracking open some beers right about now.

His gaze roamed around the room, moving from one face to the next. It only took him a few before he realized he was only searching out dark-haired women.

If he found her, he didn't know how she'd even react to seeing him. He'd never looked her up and had left her sleeping with only a note of farewell. Why hadn't he contacted her again? He knew where she lived. Sure, he had a reputation for loving and leaving women with no remorse and hardly a backward glance as he left their beds, but his thoughts had returned to Dahlia—a lot.

What were the chances he'd see her again tonight? He was a fool, but that didn't stop him from seeking out the next head of rich black hair in the crowd.

After he disregarded half a dozen more women, his heart gave a hard jerk against his ribs.

Could that be?

He circled the crowd to get a better look. Too many bodies in the way. He'd have to go in.

Carrying his drink, he stepped onto the floor, his gaze trained on the spot where he'd seen the dark beauty. She was wearing a deep red top, a color that was too close to what Dahlia had been wearing when he'd seen her last.

Actually, he'd seen that red top wadded up half under her bed on his way out, but that was beside the point.

Someone jostled him from behind, and the whiskey in the bottom of his glass sloshed over his fingers. He raised the glass and swallowed the rest and then passed his empty glass to a dancer.

She looked at it, back to him, smiled and continued dancing, still holding the glass.

Ben placed his hand on a guy's shoulder and moved him aside so he could pass. By the time he reached the spot where he'd seen the woman, she was no longer standing there.

He was tall, had the advantage at six-three of towering over most men. But Dahlia was much more petite and could easily be hidden by so many bodies. If she was here at all.

Last time they'd been together, he'd been coming off his stint in North Korea. Missions didn't make him flighty — coming back and joining civilization did. He had trouble transitioning, working out how he fit in after the shit he'd seen or done. Tonight being the perfect example.

His mind had been pretty blown up with details of the mission, and Dahlia had managed to wipe it to a blank slate with a single stroke of her silky-soft, talented fingers. Not to mention that sweet mouth and all the things it was capable of.

Great, now he was sporting wood again. He stepped around a group of dancers and spotted the dark hair that had fallen like a sheet around them as she rode him well into the night. The curve of creamy shoulder.

He closed his fingers on that shoulder and she spun to him, tipping her head all the way back to see his face.

Arousal hit his system like a fucking SS missile, along with a blast of something that felt uncomfortably like relief. Her eyes were the same deep chocolate that he'd fallen into before, and no, nothing about her appearance had been exaggerated by his brain. She was even more beautiful, if that was possible.

He breathed out a word, knowing she wouldn't hear above the music, but he needed to say it anyway. "Dahlia."

* * * * *

All night long, Dahlia'd been giving herself pep talks. She was not going to see Ben, so just forget it. She wasn't here to go home with somebody, only to meet a few new people to hang with and fill her boring evening.

Now he was standing right in front of her, looking bigger, stronger and more bad-ass than she remembered.

Before she could overcome the reaction of her body at seeing him, she caught a whiff of his aftershave, though he didn't appear to have shaved in a week. She'd stopped dancing and stood there stupidly staring up at him. They were the only two people on the dance floor standing dead still.

He still held onto her shoulder and squeezed it as he leaned in. "Can I buy you a drink?"

Not "Can we talk about me leaving before you woke." Not "I never even asked for your number."

She gave herself the fifth pep talk of the night. You're not going home with Ben.

But her body had other ideas, if the heat pooling in her lower belly and slipping down between her legs was any indication.

She nodded. and he didn't hesitate. Sliding his hand down her arm, he caught her by the hand and towed her through the group of people. If she'd tried to leave the dance floor on her own, it would have taken her fifteen minutes of pushing and excusing herself to get by, but the mass parted for Ben and closed the gap behind her.

Her mind was going haywire with the messages it was receiving. Her body was already screaming to be with this huge Cajun. To have him backing her against a wall and hemming her in with his broad chest. Crushing her lips beneath his, taking control as he had all those months ago.

But her brain was trying to wrap itself around some logic. She wasn't sleeping with him again. No way. She had some self-respect, and while they'd both enjoyed the experience—well at least she thought he had—she wasn't going for round two.

He led her to the back of the club where you could hold a conversation, but all the tables were full. Instead of turning around like any other human on the planet, Ben marched up to a table and flicked his head at the patrons.

They stared at him for a second before getting up and leaving.

Holy shit. That was arrogant as hell.

And it had worked.

The man was very different from anybody she'd ever known, which was saying a lot since she'd grown up with a father in the military.

Ben turned to her, eyes burning. More green than hazel, she remembered, but tonight they looked darker. Maybe it was the club lighting or the way they burned when he stared down at her.

He waved a hand for her to sit and after she did, he hovered over her, his mouth close to her ear. "I'll get us drinks."

Damn, her reaction time was slow tonight. If she didn't know better, she'd think herself concussed.

Oh, she had been hit in the head, all right. Struck stupid by a hot man who'd done things to her body that—

Before she could complete the thought, Ben was back, setting two drinks on the table and then taking his seat across from her.

She blinked at the drinks. "How did you get to the bar that fast? It's way up front."

"I didn't. I took these off the waitress. I hope you don't mind Sazerac."

She shook her head. The drink was undeniably New Orleans, the equivalent of a whiskey cocktail. She lifted her gaze to his, and electric sparks flew between them.

Fuck, she was hoping that life-shattering attraction wouldn't be present between them, but it was already smoldering.

Ben sat straight in his seat, gaze moving over her face and hair, over her shoulders and down to her breasts then back up to meet her eyes. "I didn't know if I'd find you here tonight. I haven't been back since we met."

"I haven't been back either."

His eyes hooded. Need spiked in her core. He was looking at her the same way he had right before he'd stripped her. She'd never forget it, and her body sure wasn't letting her now.

To cover the quiver in her belly, she picked up her drink. The cognac slipped down her throat, a warm burn all the way to her stomach. When she ran her tongue over her lips to gather the drops off, his gaze shot to her mouth and locked there.

The quiver amplified.

"Damn, it's good to set eyes on you." His gruff voice barely projected over the noise of the club, but she heard, her every sense attuned to this man. He didn't touch his drink, but she needed more liquid fortification.

Taking another sip, she floundered for something to say to him. When she lowered the glass, she managed, "Why did you come here tonight if you haven't been here besides that once?"

His stare pinned her. "To find you."

Oh God. A wave of lust and dizziness struck her, knocking her off-kilter. At this rate, she'd be flat on her back with her legs in the air, screaming Ben's name in minutes.

"Why did you come here tonight if you haven't been back either?" he asked in that warm, buttery, low drawl.

She directed a lock of dark hair over her shoulder and fought to be one of those cool women who never comes off as silly or stupid. Even though Dahlia wasn't one of them.

"I needed to unwind tonight."

His eyes sparked, tiny creases appearing around each. "So do I. What a coincidence."

She reached for her drink again, but he removed it from her clutch and wrapped her fingers gently in his big, rough hand. If she stood up, she'd be so embarrassed, because she was sure her panties had just gone up in flames and all the ash would fall out from under her skirt.

9-1-1, what's your call?

I just melted my panties. I think I'm spontaneously combusting. Please send help.

But who could help her? Under Ben's steady, smoldering stare, with her hand firmly enclosed in his, she had no choice but to follow her instincts.

And sleep with the man.

No, no—to get up and leave. She'd come to the club to unwind and now she was more high-strung than when she'd arrived.

"All I have is my bike, but there's a helmet for you. If you'll come with me."

She shook her head, an action that was becoming habit around him. He probably thought her simple-minded. They hadn't exactly exchanged a lot of words the first time around. Saliva, yes.

He reached out and snagged her other hand, holding her captive by his gaze and his touch. "Dahlia, I need you tonight."

Oh fuck.

"Will you let me take you home again? I promise we'll come back for your car in the morning."

There it was, the promise for more than waking to find your new lover gone. There would be a morning, which meant coffee, conversation, the possibility of a shower and...

Her mind was running away with her. She hadn't agreed to leaving with him.

He stroked his thumb up and down hers, circling the base in an insinuative way that had her conjuring flashes of memories of his touch all over her and his mouth slanting across hers as he sank deep into her again and again in a series of sexy man pushups.

"Dahlia," he said quietly, cocking his head and his brow at her, "don't make me beg."

At that, she laughed, the sound throaty from the cognac and desire. "As if a man like you begs."

"I can beg, but I don't want to. Just walk out that door with me, get on the back of my bike and wrap your sweet legs around me. We'll go back to your place and I'll show you how sorry I am for leaving in such a hurry before."

She didn't believe for a moment that he had a reason—she figured loving and leaving was his way. He was a playboy—his amount of game made that clear. Nobody used his eyes and words and touch like this without practice.

He drew small circles up her thumb to her nail and looked deep into her eyes. "C'mon." Without waiting for her answer, as if knowing she was already caving, he stood and drew her out of her seat. When he slid an arm around her waist and led her out of the club, it took her mind several seconds to catch up. As the cooler night air hit her hot face and the thrum of bass in her ears quieted, she realized he'd gotten her outside.

What a fool she was. She stopped walking.

"Good idea." He planted his hands on her waist and dragged her against his steely chest as he slammed his mouth over hers. He kissed like he did everything else—with total command. Her body was at his mercy as he kissed the hell out of her.

"Ben…" she murmured between sweeps of his tongue that had her toes curling in her high heels.

He drew back, face in shadow, but she saw his Adam's apple bob in his throat. "I've been thinking about you every day since we were together."

Stunned by his words, she blinked up at him. What could she say to that? The only thing on the tip of her tongue was that he'd popped into her head every day too, but she couldn't admit that, could she?

Though he just had.

If they were laying it all out on the line, she had one thing on her mind. "How can I ride a motorcycle in a skirt?"

He dipped his gaze over her body, leaving a trail of warm, sticky honey behind. "We could take it off first."

A laugh escaped her, just as throaty as before. "I don't think so. This *is* the party capital of the world, but I think the police would frown on a naked woman riding on the back of a bike unless it's Mardi Gras."

"Well, *cher*," he drawled, pressing closer to her and planting his hand on her buttocks to keep her in place, "you've had me between your thighs before. Call it a warmup."

She shivered at his words, and when he caressed her ass, hiking up the fabric of her skirt as he did, she nearly came on the spot.

He did that incredibly hot maneuver again where he leaned close to speak into her ear without turning his lips to it. "What do you say?"

She felt herself nod.

Walking across gravel in heels was never an easy task, let alone when one had knees of jelly. Why the club didn't pave the parking lot was beyond her, probably thought it lent to the authenticity or something.

Dahlia could barely remain upright but somehow made it to his bike. She expected something polished, shiny and new. Instead, Ben's motorcycle was vintage, looking to be from the '50s at least.

He shot her a crooked smile that felt like syrup dripping over her body as he mounted the bike in a slow, deliberate maneuver and kickstarted it. Then he handed her the helmet, which she strapped under her chin, the long hair she'd released from the confines of her bun after work trapped around her neck and shoulders.

Ben tipped his head for her to get on the back, and she did, obviously giving him a show when her skirt rode up her thighs.

"I just saw your panties, and I can't wait to take them off you," he growled. "Now put your arms around me."

Holding on to a man this big wasn't easy with short arms, but she scooted up until her pussy was pasted to his ass and she could lock her fingers together. As they rolled out of the parking lot, her mind spun. She couldn't believe she was doing this—for a second time. Where was her self-respect?

Who cared? He was the sexiest thing on two legs, and she wasn't going to miss another chance to be in his bed. Opportunities like this didn't happen more than once in a lifetime, and anything else was baby angels raining golden gifts down upon her.

When they hit the asphalt, he gassed the bike and they shot forward. Dahlia squealed and felt his rumbling laugh vibrating through her arms and body. She wiggled closer, and he tossed her a look as they took the streets of New Orleans at a pace that suggested maybe he was just as eager to be with her.

* * * * *

They fell through her door, and he kicked it shut, reaching back to twist the deadbolt. The sexy vixen was all over him, her arms around his neck and her body plastered to his. He lifted her, and she wrapped her thighs high on his hips.

"You know the way," she said in that sultry voice that was quickly stripping away his control. His balls ached and his cock throbbed as he navigated her dark apartment.

Her bedroom door was open, her ceiling fan revolving slowly and providing a trickle of cool air. His mouth watered as he lay her on her bed and followed her down. When he claimed her lips, his heart gave an odd undulation of excitement. He'd been with women over the course of the months, but he needed to get back between the thighs of this one particular woman.

To sink into her hot, tight body and lose his mind.

She plucked at the cotton of his T-shirt on his spine, and he rolled his shoulders to help her strip it over his head. She threw the garment aside and he dived for her neck as she ran her hands over his pecs.

"This is crazy," she gasped as he dotted kisses up the column of her throat and bit into her ear right above her dangly earring.

"It's crazier not to follow our instincts." He scraped his teeth down her neck again, and she squirmed in his hold. When he reached her collarbone, he lapped lightly at the delicate line, following it to the hollow of her throat and finally lower to her cleavage.

Dragging in a deep breath, his head flooded with her unique scent and the traces of her perfume, the same as she'd worn before. He ran his nose up and down the seam of her breasts and considered shredding her top to get at what was underneath.

"What is that maddening scent?" he murmured.

She named a perfume he didn't know but would definitely remember. It was all woman, all Dahlia. As he scraped his jaw over her blouse to her breast, his beard made a scratching noise against the cloth. He flattened his palm over her stomach, easily able to span her waist with his long reach of fingers. He'd forgotten how petite she was, how fucking perfect.

He pushed back to look down at her. "I need you naked. Now."

She bit into her lower lip and he issued a low groan, his mind running with the memory of what her sharp little teeth had left all over his chest and abs that night. He'd worn her marks for most of a week.

He reached for her hem and she sat up as he pulled off her shirt. Her bra clasp took a simple pinch of his fingers to release.

"You're damn good at that. Practice much?" She cocked a dark, arching brow at him, and he couldn't help the crooked smile that claimed his mouth.

Pressing on his shoulders, she got him on the mattress and rolled atop him. With her skirt bunched around her hips, her pussy nestled over his bulging erection. Thank God his jeans acted as a barrier, because if they were skin to skin, he would have lost it by now.

Need pulsated through his system. This was what he'd been hoping for—her to dissolve that stress and turn his memories of the compound into smoke. With Dahlia, there was nothing but this... *wanting*.

She leaned over him, hair tumbling around them in thick waves the way he remembered, and he wished to hell he had more hands. Sinking his fingers into her hair and cradling her head, he inched his other hand up her smooth, bare thigh to her ass. He let out a groan as he discovered just how high her panties rode up on her full ass. She may be small but she was packed with curves.

"Fuck." He hooked his fingers under the elastic of the leg and followed the cloth up to her hip. She

42

ground against him, breath washing over his lips and tormenting him further. "I'm not going to make it long if I don't take you."

She swished her pussy back and forth over his erection in a teasing way that had him gritting his teeth. "Nobody's holding you back."

He flipped her. Sucked her breasts into hard peaks until she was writhing and then dragged his rough jaw down the center of her body, leaving red beard burn in his wake. This time he wanted *her* wearing *his* marks.

Her skirt took half a second to discard, and he had intentions of ripping her panties, but once he spotted the expensive white lingerie, he couldn't bring himself to rip them off. He wanted to see them on her again too bad.

Lowering his head, he caught the thin floss of silk in his teeth and edged them down inch by inch, holding her gaze as he did. His cock swelled to the point of bursting, but he wasn't going to shuck his jeans until the last second.

Goosebumps rose on her skin as he tugged her panties off with his teeth. Inch by inch they slid off. Once she was free, he started at those ankles he remembered so well. Licking the smooth skin, moving up her calves and stopping at her inner thighs. Her scents of arousal had him drunker than any amount of whiskey he could down, and damn if she wasn't glistening with need.

43

From between her legs, he looked up at her. Her stomach dipped sharply, and her breasts heaved with her labored breathing.

"Ben," she rasped.

He held her gaze and without warning, speared her pussy with two fingers. Slamming deep, enveloped to the knuckles by her fiery heat. Need exploded in him, and he had to close his eyes against the sweet torture as he pressed his fingertips upward into her inner wall. Juices flooded his hand, and she went wild. Sharp cries escaped her plump lips as she bucked her hips, pushing up and down on his fingers to get what she needed so badly.

With his other hand, he reached up her body to close his fingers over her nipple as he slowly, gently eased his fingers out of her body. "More," she whimpered, but he was going at this at his own pace, the way he did everything.

Watching her beautiful features, he filled her pussy with his fingers one more time. And again. She shuddered in pleasure. Fucking her slowly, he kept her just on the edge.

Her inner walls squeezed his digits and when he felt the first pulsation of her orgasm starting, he pulled his fingers free.

"Oh God. Ben, don't stop." She'd bitten her lips so they were swollen and wine-red. He moved up her body to paint her full lower lip with her own juices. Her mouth parted on a gasp and he kissed her hard, lapping at her flavors, sinking his tongue deep in mimicry of his fingers in her pussy.

She clung to him with one arm around his shoulders and reached between them to pop the button of his jeans. The zipper vibration set his teeth on edge and sent his cock pounding in time to his pulse. When she reached inside his briefs and pulled out his cock, he shuddered.

There was nothing but Dahlia—that compound wasn't even on the map of his mind anymore.

He got to his knees and fisted his shaft, watching her eyelids flutter as she looked on. Fuck yeah, he remembered that from the first time—she enjoyed watching him stroke himself.

"You like that, don't you? You want to see me get off for you?"

"Yesss," she hissed.

"Maybe later. Right now, I want your legs spread wide on this bed while I put on a condom."

He didn't need to ask her twice. As he got to his feet and removed his boots, socks and kicked off his jeans and briefs, his sultry woman didn't just part her thighs a little bit—she spread them as wide as he expected.

The sight was too much, and he couldn't stare too long or he'd risk blowing too soon. He ripped open a condom and rolled it in place with one jerk of his hand. Fuck, he hated these things, so confining. And he wanted to feel Dahlia wrapped around him with no barriers, only her extreme heat and his balls resting against her ass as he sank to the root.

She slid her hands down her body, letting him see how she touched herself. Sometime soon they would have to play. But not tonight. He hovered over her again, nuzzling her lips as he ran his cock head up and down her slick seam.

"Ben, I want this so bad. Don't make me wait."

Now there was no holding back. He thrust in hard, and she cried out. Tossing her head back on the pillow, stretching perfectly around him. He lowered his mouth to her throat, tasting the sweetness of her skin and moving upward over her jaw to the corner of her lips.

When she twisted her mouth against his and kissed him with so much pent-up passion, he let go of his firm grip on control and his body guided him.

In boot camp, they practiced shooting and tactical maneuvers over and over until it was reflex. This was something much more primal, a drive to sink into Dahlia completely and never surface.

He jerked his hips, she raised hers to meet his plunges. Their tongues tangled, and he heard his unintelligible words that she answered with breathy ones of her own. The darkness of her apartment, the scent of her perfume, the cool air of the overhead fan on his sweat-dotted spine all heightened his awareness far too fast.

Leaning back, he met her eyes, glossy with pleasure. He had to watch her shatter for him and fast. Had to feel her pulsating around him before he could let go of his precious grip on control and come.

She dug her short nails into his ass, dragging him down, closer, harder. The bed shook as he claimed her with everything in him. And she gave herself up.

A sharp cry left her as a mind-blowing first hard pulse of her pussy around his length stripped away his control.

"Holy fuck," he ground out as her second contraction hit. A rough cry escaped her, and her next clench sent him over the edge. Heat blasted up from his spine to envelop him.

All thought fled as he let go completely, pounding into her, staking his claim in her body as a roar shook his chest and long seconds passed. Scorching heat tore through him as each spurt left his body.

His mind blank, he collapsed. When he finally drifted back to reality, it was to soft kisses being rained all over his face, eyelids and finally his mouth.

"Dahlia," he breathed for the second time that night, cupping her cheek.

Chapter Three

"I must be crazy," she murmured, turning on her side as Ben got out of bed to deal with the condom. Her skin burned from his touch and the sear of his rough beard on her. And her insides still hummed with the pleasure of their coupling.

But yeah, she'd lost her mind. She stared at the bathroom door, waiting for him to come back — if he came back. For all she knew, he'd climb out the tiny window and escape.

That was unlikely, she told herself. And if he came back, would he want to do the post-coitus cuddling session?

Ugh, she was already a wreck. She *knew* Ben was no good for her, yet she'd let her libido take over every single one of her brain cells. Tomorrow how was she going to do her job and do it well? People depended on her to keep them safe and save lives, and she'd be so caught up in memories of... this... that she didn't know if she could think straight.

The crack of the door opening almost gave her heart failure, and she jerked the covers up to her chin. His gaze fell over her, and damn if she didn't feel the heat of it.

He returned to the bed and she felt the mattress give under his bulky weight. He curled around her, his mouth at her ear again. "You all right, honey?"

Did he have to smell so good, feel amazing and have the perfect tone of sweetness? It would be easier to kick him out of her bed if he was a jackass.

Maybe if she feigned sleep, he'd just leave. She wouldn't put it past him to go against his word to stay till morning anyway.

He trailed his lips across her shoulder, raising the hairs on her neck. "You never told me your middle name."

She twitched and rolled to her back to stare at him. "You remember that conversation?"

"I remember everything about that night." He tapped his temple in a way that told her he didn't forget much. "You know my middle name. I think it's only fair for you to tell me yours." He brushed his lips over the crest of her shoulder again.

"Yours is Bartholomew." Though she didn't know his last name, she did know that he had a slew of crazy brothers and sisters and was oldest. Other than that, she knew he had a penchant for crawfish and grits, but what self-respecting Louisianan didn't?

He nodded, eyes shining. So green they reminded her of picnics and long hikes—two things she'd never be doing with Benjamin Bartholomew Whatever-His-Name-Was.

She gnawed on her lower lip until he pressed the pad of his thumb against it, removing it from her teeth. She pushed out a sigh. "My middle name's nothing special. It's Ann, after my mother."

His smile was something straight off the glossy cover of a magazine—part bad boy, part movie star.

"No last names though," she insisted.

His eyes darkened as if he didn't like her condition, but he only nodded. "Fine."

"Since we're sharing, what do you do for a living?" If he was staying, he was giving more details. *Then at least my imagination would have more to play with.*

A crease appeared between his brows. When he didn't answer, she said, "With all these muscles, it could be construction."

His brows smoothed.

"Am I right?"

"More like destruction. Demolition."

Her hands had a mind of their own and roved over his muscled shoulders and hard pecs. When she reached the base of his abs, close to his stiff cock, he stopped her with a hand on her wrist.

"Before I let you have your way with me, you have to tell me what *you* do for a living." His eyes burned into her, and she swore when she got off this bed, she'd find scorch marks outlining where she'd lain on the sheets.

"I'm a 911 operator."

Interest sparked in his eyes. "Are you?"

"Yes. And I had a rough day at work that I need to forget. Now let me use you to forget." She slithered down his body, landing kisses over his hard chest and flicking her tongue around one nipple to the sound of his groan.

Then she made her way down to the ripples of his abs. Licking each and every swell was the stuff women dreamed of when they looked at him, she was sure of it. She didn't want to think of how many had navigated this chiseled landscape before her, and continued exploring until she reached his cock.

He lay on his back, one arm slung behind his head in a pose that looked far too casual for the tension she felt humming just under his skin. She flashed a glance at him and snaked out her tongue, tasting the spongy tip of his cock where the sweetness pooled.

His eyes drifted shut and a moan left him.

Feeling the power of having him at her mercy, she went on, swirling her tongue around and around the tip and then gliding it down the underside to the base.

Ben jerked his hips. "Fuck," he bit off.

"Oh, we will, babe. Right after I drive you a little bit crazy." When she opened her mouth wide and sucked him right to the back of her throat, he fisted the sheets.

"Jesus. A little bit?"

She reveled in the handsome, rugged man unraveling at the suction of her mouth and the pull of her lips. She bobbed down and then back up. As she lowered her head again, he dropped his hand to her nape and pushed her all the way down. With one hand wrapped around his base, she was able to control how deep she took him into her mouth, but she pressed farther, wanting to give him something to remember.

"Ffffuck." He shuddered, thighs stiff and bulging with muscle.

Flipping her tongue around his shaft like she was licking an ice cream cone, she made her way back to the tip and moaned as his salty-sweet juice hit her tongue.

He cracked an eye at her as she lapped at his slit.

"Enough. You're killin' me, woman." He wrapped her hair around his fist and guided her back up. The sting on her scalp only heightened her arousal. She leaned off the side of the mattress and grabbed a condom from her nightstand drawer.

He cocked a brow at her. "I don't know if it's sexy as hell that you're prepared or I'm jealous."

She only smiled sweetly. Straddling his thighs, she worked the rubber down his veined shaft, throwing him coy looks as she did.

"You know exactly what you're fucking doing to me," he ground out.

She caught her lip in her teeth again and released it. "Maybe."

He grabbed her ass and shoved her over his erection. Oh God, this man had enough sex appeal to make a woman explode. She didn't want to thrust up and down like a wanton, but if this was the last moment she ever had with Ben, she was damn well getting her money's worth.

Cupping her ass cheeks, spreading them slightly, he guided her down a little more. They shared a noise of ecstasy, but he was watching her too closely. What was he up to?

When he parted her cheeks farther and skimmed a forefinger over her netherhole, she sucked in a gasp. Liquid heat dumped into her core. Holy hell… She tested a movement, causing his fingertip to skim her most private region.

She gasped. Nobody had ever touched her there, but it was soooo good. Of course it *would* be Ben to open those doors to her. A man she couldn't have or couldn't keep.

He slid his finger along the outer ring of her pucker, and a throaty noise broke from her.

Her gaze flew to his and their eyes locked. She sank another fraction down his cock, and he caressed her unexplored pucker again, a light tease of his fingertip that was doing unspeakable things to her insides.

Quivering now, she waited for his next move. Would he try to break through her barriers and slide his finger into her ass? Did she want him to?

Yes, she did.

She pushed backward and managed to slip down his erection more.

"Hell," he grated out and pressed on her netherhole. His fingertip sank inside her, and pleasure rushed up. She couldn't stop herself from moving—had to or die.

She slammed over him, and fuck—the man was good, all right. He sank his finger all the way inside.

The burning pleasure washed over her, and she barely had a second to adjust before he rocked his hips and withdrew his finger simultaneously.

Ben was one dirty lover, and damn she wanted more. She moaned and hung there over him, unable to for a coherent thought around the insane pleasure coursing through her system.

Realizing she was boneless, he took control, moving his hips up and down, his cock stretching and filling her to the fullest capacity even as his finger had breached new territory.

"God, you're so responsive. I should have known. Dammit, Dahlia." He spoke as if her being responsive annoyed him, but right this second she couldn't care less—she only wanted to reach that invisible summit he was pushing her toward.

He fucked his finger in and out in time to his thrusts, and suddenly it wasn't enough. She needed to move too.

Using her thigh muscles, she rocked up and down on his muscled hips, taking him all the way and forcing his finger right where she wanted it—deep.

"Has anybody ever fucked you here before?" His gaze trained on her face, sweat beading his forehead.

She shook her head, sending her hair flying around them. "Never."

"A virgin. Dammit to hell." He moved his finger, stretching her to the point of no return. A deep thrum had taken up residence inside her, and she could feel a brand-new flutter she'd never experienced before.

"That's it. Clamp down on me. Fuck, you feel so good."

Need pulsated through her, making her hot, cold, tingly, numb. She had no idea where her body was going with this, but it was like being on a speeding train with no tracks in sight or straddling a runaway horse. Either way, she was crashing at the end, and she had a feeling she'd never be the same after this experience.

Her throaty cries grew louder, harsher. He moaned in response, and soon the room echoed with their noises of pleasure. He stiffened, jerking his hips faster. His fingertip was hitting that spot even as his cock hit another erogenous zone.

There was no going back, but suddenly panic hit her.

"Ben?" The confusion of what was about to happen to her made his name come out as a question.

"I got you, honey. Just let go."

She looked into his eyes, being pushed over a cliff into the unknown. Her entire body racked with orgasm, her insides clenching and releasing wildly, her juices drenching them both. He continued to thrust upward and used his finger on her backside, stealing all breath, all thought.

She screamed, and he locked an arm around her, yanking her down for his kiss as his own release hit. Her mind locked to his warmth, the feel of his strength grounding her. The need pulsing through her body didn't die down even a little bit as he found her mouth and took control of a kiss.

A raucous final cry rushed up her throat and shivers gripped her. He slowed his pace, withdrew his finger. She collapsed to the side and he pulled her into his arms, tucking her head beneath his chin. After a moment or two she drifted and felt him get up to use the bathroom. By the time he returned and pulled her tightly against his chest, she knew she was half in love.

No, not love. Lust. Nobody fell in love with a man after two screws, even if he was a master with his fingers and cock.

She'd like to put his tongue to the test. That shower in the morning was looking more and more exciting.

The smooth swaths of his palm on her back made her relax and drift. Her long day was catching up to her, but more so she found he'd fucked the energy right out of her. Under her ear, his heart thudded, strong and true.

"Dahlia." His low voice penetrated her sexual haze.

"Hmm?"

"I'm glad you were in that club tonight."

"Me too."

He drew her closer, his breath warm against her skin. Odd how comfortable she felt sleeping against this man, a virtual stranger. Surely that was odd...

Hours later, she woke to daylight streaming over her bed—her empty bed. She pushed to her elbows, straining to hear the shower or her lover banging around the kitchen to fix coffee. But the apartment was silent, Ben was nowhere around and there was a note on her nightstand.

With a groan, she jerked into a sitting position and snatched up the note.

Dahlia,

I'm sorry I went back on my word and couldn't stay till morning. I've had someone collect your car and you'll find it parked out front. Next time we meet at the club, I promise to clear my schedule.

B-

She crumpled the note in her fist. "Son of a bitch. That's two strikes, Ben. And you don't get a third." Too bad her body was already latched onto the idea of a next time and the man's yummy scent clung to her and her sheets.

* * * * *

"Whose car was that anyway?" Sean's question didn't even warrant a response from Ben. He was too involved in keeping watch through his binoculars. The wet sand clung to his black clothes and dampness seeped in, making him even more pissed off that he'd been dragged from Dahlia's bed and into this mission.

Sean elbowed him. "The car?"

He grunted. "You're not gonna let this go, are you? It's a friend's. Thanks for picking it up for me."

"It was fun. I haven't hotwired anything in years."

"Knew you'd enjoy yourself." He paused. "Give the signal. I see it."

Sean scooted closer in the divot they'd dug in the sandy beach to conceal themselves. "You have eyes on the craft?"

"I see a light and it's growing closer." His words were soft but deadly. When he'd received the urgent call that he was to meet his brothers to intercept a vessel rumored to be carrying enough cocaine to give all of the French Quarter a buzz for days, he'd been pissed. Climbing out of Dahlia's bed, leaving her sleeping so peacefully, her dark hair streaming over her creamy skin… Hell, she'd probably never let him in her bed again.

Who could blame her?

Why the hell the DEA wasn't handling the drug trafficking case was his first question put to Colonel Jackson. Apparently, in addition to the drugs, a known hunted terrorist was also among the cargo. That had gotten Ben scrambling pretty quick.

Sean gave the signal, a flash of a mirror that the rest of the Knight Ops team could detect but was in the opposite direction of the incoming craft.

"Tell our team to sit tight. The light's coming nearer." Ben barely breathed out the message.

Two flicks of Sean's mirror had them on the ready. Their operative — to let the drug runners reach the shore and use darkness on their side. They were trained for stealth and boarding that watercraft wouldn't be any difficult matter. Though they had no clue who may be guarding the criminal trying to slip into the country, Ben was confident that his men could stop anything that came their way.

The best possible outcome was that everything went peaceably, with no gunfire exchanged and no boat explosions.

Though blowing shit up sounded right up his alley at the moment. The fuckers had yanked him from Dahlia's bed, dammit, and she was never going to understand because he couldn't explain it to her.

A metallic click sounded, and he and Sean scrambled, twisting in the sand, training their sights on the man moving through the darkness like nothing more than a shadow.

"Easy, Knight Ops. Rocko reporting for duty."

"Jesus Christ, Rocko. About time you joined us, but you have piss-poor timing." Ben lowered his weapon and grabbed his binoculars again as the sixth man of their team who'd missed out on all the fun of the compound raid landed in the sand next to them.

"Sorry I'm late, Captain."

"You'll make it up to me, don't worry," Ben grated out, low. He scanned the water, right, left, right, left, and couldn't see the goddamn boat. "Dammit, it's disappeared."

"Probably spotted a man on shore and booked it out of here," Sean added.

"Bullshit. No one saw me," Rocko scoffed, amusement in his tone. "He's still out there, just circling. It's what illegals do when approaching shores. Take it from a SEAL." He pulled out his own binoculars and trained them on the inky black water, the small waves stronger with the night winds.

Each time Rocko shifted, his shoulder rubbed against Ben's. "This is one hell of a way to meet our sixth team member. I don't even know you and we're already cuddling."

Ignoring him, a heartbeat of silence passed and then Rocko said, "I got eyes on it." He gave a hand signal that the boat was two hundred yards to the left offshore. "We're in the wrong position."

"We've got it covered. Rocko and Thunder, you keep the lookout and wait for my command." Ben belly-crawled away for a few yards before getting into a crouch and rushing through the darkness to meet up with the other half of his team.

Behind him, he heard Rocko say to Sean, "Thunder? That you?"

Ben gave a mental shake of his head. He was going to have to bring this kid up to speed on their team. He didn't even know the nicknames of his fellow members, and there was no excuse for not doing his homework. Rocko should know everything from what each Knight brother ate for breakfast down to his ammo of choice, and he had damn well better know the names and appearance of every terrorist on the planet too.

Ben waded into the water, moving in a way that would reduce waves and keep them from lapping against the boat where his men waited.

61

"Thunder?" Dylan whispered.

"Nope. He's back with that squid."

"Squid? Rocko showed up?" Dylan moved aside as Ben pulled himself silently up and into the boat. Water streamed off him, and he looked to the shore for his team's signal.

Nothing came. He had a second to explain.

"He apologized for being delayed and said he'd make it up to me."

"Good thing. The Knight Mobile needs cleaned."

A huff of a laugh came from Chaz, who'd most likely caused most of the mess in the SUV with food wrappers and empty energy drink cans.

Ben swung his gaze between the water and the sand. "Nothing yet," he said quietly.

"We have time for the story then," Roades said.

Ben looked at him. The moon was nonexistent tonight, a perfect night for a delivery of goods on US soil. But it meant his youngest brother couldn't see his glare.

"No story tonight."

"Aw, c'mon, Ma. Just one?" Roades always was a whiner at bedtime, but since he was the youngest, he'd often gotten their *maman* to read one more story.

"Nothing to tell." Ben knew what they were after.

"When we're instructed to stop at a club, hotwire a woman's car and drive it to an unknown locale, then it's a story. Who is she?" Roades pushed.

62

"None of your fucking business. Now where—Fuck!"

They all went on high alert, scanning both water and sand. Ben twitched two fingers in the direction of the van rolling across the sand, dangerously close to where Sean and Rocko lay.

"Transport's here," Ben said. "Hope to hell this doesn't go sideways."

Dylan's teeth flashed white with his self-assured smile. "Not fucking likely, bro."

"Time to move." Ben slipped back overboard, along with Dylan. Leaving two on the sand, two at sea and them in the middle, covering all angles. As the boat drifted into sight, the doors of the van opened and closed. But through the darkness, Ben couldn't see a single man leave the vehicle.

Because they were already on the ground, gagged and bound, if Sean and Rocko had done their jobs properly.

A quiet call came from the approaching craft, followed by a splash as a man dropped overboard. Ben raised an arm, a reflector in his hand giving his men the signal. Chaz and Roades started the engine and shouts sounded from the drug runners. But it was too late, because he and Dylan had reached the craft and Rocko joined up with them while Sean guarded the prisoners.

In minutes, Knight Ops had five men trussed up like pigs for Sunday dinner on the beach and half a

63

mil in cocaine seized. Not to mention an overlord of terrorism who could have let dozens more just like him into the country in custody.

"Here comes the DEA now." Chaz flicked his head toward the vans with DEA painted in white letters on the sides.

"Hm, what gives you the impression it's the DEA?" Ben drawled. Maybe if they could pass these criminals off to their counterparts quickly, he could hurry back to Dahlia and slip into her bed before dawn.

He looked at the horizon. Fat chance. A pale band of light appeared between sky and sea. He compressed his lips.

"You in charge here?" A woman in slim cargo pants and a dark jacket stormed across the sand to Ben.

"Uh, I am," Chaz tried to lure her away as usual.

She threw him a look that could shrivel any man's balls, but Knights were made of tougher stuff and Chaz just chuckled.

Ben jerked his jaw upward. "That's me. Let's make this quick. I've got someplace to be."

"I need to know who authorized you."

"Well, if I tell you that, I'd have to kill you." Ben wasn't putting up with some harpy on a power trip. A deep ache to feel Dahlia in his arms again had taken up residence in his core.

"You military types are so funny," the DEA woman said with a tinkle of a laugh that had Chaz's head whipping. She gestured to the men lying like sardines on the beach along with a few crates of cocaine. The rest of the drugs was still in the hull of their vessel. "Load everyone and everything into the vans while I deal with this matter," she ordered her men. She turned back to Ben.

"Look, lady, I don't answer to you. You know who sent us and why."

Ben didn't have much time, and he still had to debrief and unload this terrorist onto his superiors. He sighed. More hours of bullshit talk and forms filled out. More hours spent away from Dahlia, if he returned to her at all.

"Sean, make the call so we can get this show on the road." He raised a hand and his men fell in around him. They started away with the terrorist in tow. Over his shoulder, he said to the DEA agent in charge, "By the way, that's your boat we borrowed to do our jobs. Hope you don't mind loading it back onto the trailer. Thanks."

For the next hour and long into the morning, the guys joked about how Ben had ticked off that woman, but he could only think about the dark-haired beauty he'd left behind and whether or not he'd ever get another chance with her.

Chapter Four

Two weeks. Two weeks since Dahlia'd slept with Ben, so why couldn't she shake the feeling that he'd just spread her thighs and —

She cut off the thought for the thousandth time since waking to find him gone, more pissed than she'd ever been, and it wasn't Ben she was mad at. After all, he was just a man, right? And men played. He'd proven he was a player from the start, yet she'd given him a second chance. This was where lust got her.

She'd wanted the big man with a burning desire and had let herself get carried away. But now she was just angry and disappointed with herself. Not for giving him another romp in her bed, but because this time she'd let herself get too entangled.

Maybe she was just lonely. Her girlfriends had abandoned her for new husbands and new lives, and she definitely needed to find a new crowd but hadn't returned to the club since that night she'd found Ben again. For two weeks she'd been going home after work. She'd been trying to find new outlets for her stress but no amount of yoga downward dog or salutes to the sun were going to erase all the haunting calls she received in a regular shift.

Picking up her knitting needles, she attacked the wool again.

"How long are you making that thing, Dahlia?" Joanie asked from her desk.

She glanced up at her coworker, saw the worry written between the woman's brows and threw the knitting back into her bag. "You're right. I need to end it." Her mind wasn't on the project so much as what was going on inside her. Ben had walked out of her life, but he'd left a note behind with enough hope in the words to drive Dahlia batshit crazy.

She had to end whatever fantasy was going on in her mind.

Her earpiece buzzed, alerting her to a call. "9-1-1, what's your call?"

"I know you told me not to call you here but it's an emergency, Dahlia." Serena's voice projected into her ear.

Damn. She looked around for Kyle but didn't see her boss lurking around.

"Fine, what's your emergency?" she said urgently.

"Mike's buddy's in town and we want to double date."

She glared at nothing in particular. "A double date? That's your emergency?" She was getting more and more irritated with her friend. Calling during her shift, clogging up the lines with crap that could get Dahlia fired.

"Yes, he's a nice guy. Pulllease? We have tickets to the game."

On the other hand, a date could take her mind off her day's work as well as block Ben from her brain.

"Fine. I'll go. Now let me get back to work. Goodbye."

When she hung up, she caught Joanie's private smile. "Sounds like a good emergency to have, dear," the woman said.

She twisted her lips in some semblance of a smile. She was feeling far from excited about the date, but at least she wasn't going home alone. Somehow, the prospect helped her get through her shift without a pity-party.

After her shift she read her text messages and learned she was meeting her friends and the blind date at the club. *The* club, the only place where she'd seen Ben.

Just pulling into the parking lot had her pulse racing. Last time she'd been here...

She snapped out of that self-destructive train of thought. And just how the hell had her car gotten to her apartment when her keys were inside her purse anyway? Ben had question marks written all over his big, hunky body but she wasn't going to dwell on the hotness of a mystery.

She parked the car and reached into her big bag. Inside, she kept an array of accessories needed to amp up her daytime look for night. From sparkly necklaces to high heels and all the flirty lipstick colors between.

Dahlia was a master of parking lot makeovers, and in seconds she went from frumpy 911 operator to date night ready. Hair fluffed, lips outlined in her trademark red lipstick, her comfy shoes ditched for stilettos with rhinestones on the toes and a cute velvet top pulled over her tank top. She got out of the car.

As soon as she glanced toward the entrance, her heart skidded to a stop. Her hand few to her chest and no wonder—she needed chest compressions to restart it.

Ben was leaning against a black SUV that looked big enough to haul a team of linebackers.

He drew away from the SUV and started toward her, big thighs straining against his jeans ohhh, so right. Her pussy clenched at the mere sight of all that testosterone headed her way.

When he stopped before her, he flicked his gaze down her body, lingering around her ankles before coming back up to settle on her face. "I see you got dressed up for me."

She found her voice. "Arrogant ass. Who are you to assume that I'm here to see you?"

And just how was he finding her so easily? Could this really be coincidence?

Taking a step toward her, he let his eyes hood in that way that drove her absolutely crazy with desire.

She curled her toes in her rhinestone stilettos and attempted to slow her breathing.

"Look, Dahlia, I'm sorry for—"

She waved a hand, cutting him off. "It was nothing. Just a one-night stand."

A growl left him, so low and rumbly that she nearly threw herself into his arms there and then. "A one-night stand? Is that what you think?"

"That's what it was—twice. So if you'll let me past you, I have to get inside." She had to actually take steps toward the gorgeous man she'd been dreaming about for weeks in order to reach the door. Which meant ungluing her feet from the parking lot and putting one in front of the other. She took a step.

He caught her elbow as tried to pass and drove her crazier by placing his lips inches from her ear. "It wasn't just a one-night stand. Or even a two-night stand, honey."

Shivers raced up and down her spine and tingles started between her thighs.

"Let me take you out on a date. But not here. Someplace nice."

"I…" Her throat closed on the need to respond with a loud, resounding *yes*.

No, she couldn't go anywhere with him. He was toxic, just as poisonous to her mindset as losing a patient over the phone was.

She shook her head. "I have a date waiting for me inside."

Instead of releasing her arm as she expected, he gripped it tighter and swayed her into him, totally overstepping all her boundaries.

"A date?"

She didn't need to glance at his expression to know he didn't like what she'd said. His tone said it all.

"Look, Ben, you've been gone for two weeks. You know where I live, could have contacted me any time. But you didn't, and I have a date."

"The hell you do." He spun her against his chest and lowered his lips until they hovered over hers. Need pounded in her veins and much, much lower as his scent enveloped her. Why the hell were there so many pheromones at play? As if she needed another reason to be attracted to the man, her body was picking up whatever invisible waves he was tossing out at her.

She swallowed hard. "Please let me go." Her words wobbled, and she didn't sound one bit convincing.

His green eyes burned. "You don't really want that, *cher*."

"I... do. Ben, I have a da—"

He silenced her with his kiss. Firm lips trapping hers. She made the mistake of dragging in a deep breath of his delicious male scent.

Her knees threatened to give out.

He worked his lips over hers until she parted them on a soft sigh. To her surprise, he didn't sweep his tongue inside, which left her throbbing, aching, smoldering for more.

Damn him.

"You have to come with me." Why did his low voice have to reach inside and tug on her ovaries?

She opened her mouth to protest, but he claimed her with another deep kiss. The music coming from the club pulsed through her body as need took hold. Crap, she was a goner. She'd never hear this particular blend of zydeco and techno without thinking of Ben.

He plunged his tongue into her mouth as he lifted her and carried her to his SUV. When he pushed her against the side and cupped her ass in his big, rough hand, she made a throaty noise.

How horrible. So shameful. Yet she couldn't stop her libido from responding a hundred and fifty percent to this man.

"Ben..."

"It'll be better this time, I promise." He kissed a path up her neck to her ear. When he gently bit into her lobe, gooseflesh broke over her.

"That's what you said last time," she said between lashes of his tongue on her ear.

He held her prisoner against the side of the SUV. "Honey, I can feel how wet you are."

"How? You haven't touched me."

"Because you're so hot that I can feel it radiating from between your legs. Maybe I should check though." Holding her gaze, he eased a hand up under her skirt. When he ran a fingertip along the thin fabric covering her seam, she couldn't choke back the moan.

"Mmm, just as I thought. Soaking." He followed the cloth from her clit to her entrance and then farther back where the string of her thong disappeared between her cheeks.

"Oh God, Ben," she rasped. Her body remembered his touch back there and reminded her how much she wanted it again.

He let his fingers linger there for a heartbeat too long before sliding them up again, over the swollen lips of her pussy to settle over her clit.

He didn't press down like she wanted—needed. She panted and fought for control. What was he doing to her? She was a smart woman who knew her mind but when he got near her, her brain caved in and her body cried out for his touch.

"I can't. Ben, I really do have a date."

"Yep. With me." He edged his fingertip under her panties and skimmed her clit. The nerves leaped, and her pussy flooded. He brushed his lips across hers. "Tell me you'd rather go out with someone else, Dahlia. Say the words and I'll let you walk into that club and have your boring, polite date." He flicked her bud back and forth with his words, and her legs buckled. He pinned her to the vehicle with his body and thigh. "Or you can have this."

With that, he ground her clit into her body. She threw her head back and issued a cry that was part sexual frustration and part annoyance at her own lack of control.

He reached around her and opened the passenger door. "What do you say, Dahlia? Polite date with boring Joe-Bob or me demanding that you take off that sticky, hot thong and spread your legs for me while I drive you back to your place?"

Oh God. She threw a look at the door of the club. He was probably spot-on when it came to her date. Blind dates were never easy, and they sure as hell weren't spiked with innuendo and the promise of explosive sex like she had with Ben.

He crushed his lips down on hers again, cupping her breast and using his thigh against her pussy to prove his point.

Gasping, she tore away. "Fine. I'll get in."

The arrogant man actually smirked as he pushed off the side of the vehicle and helped her on shaky legs to the passenger's seat.

She barely hit the leather when he got behind the wheel and stared at her for a long second.

"What?" Her voice wavered.

He glanced at her thighs. "The thong—off. And spread those legs for me. I'm going to finger you as we drive. I figure I can get at least one orgasm from you before we reach our destination."

74

* * * * *

Ben wanted to go back inside that club, locate the man Dahlia had a date with and break his legs. Okay, that was going a bit far. He'd just rough him up a little. Standard black eyes, bloody nose, maybe a loose tooth or two.

His eyes hooded as he watched her squirming in the seat next to him.

"The thong, Dahlia."

"Oh God," she murmured.

He ran a finger up her thigh. "Or I'll rip them off you."

"Fine. Don't rip them. I like these ones." She shot him a look that was too heated to be a glare and reached under her skirt. She shimmied her thong down her thighs.

"All the way off."

She did his bidding, and the string caught on her high heel.

"Leave it. It's kinda sexy." He leaned over the console to eye the tangle of lace and silk around the spike heel.

"Now let me feel this wet pussy." Without hesitation, he reached under her skirt and cupped her steaming hot, drenched flesh.

"Oh my God!" she cried out.

He reached over with his left hand to put the SUV into drive and probed her silken folds with his right

75

while bumping out of the gravel lot. Need slashed through him, sugarcoating the high he was on after she'd given up her date for him.

When they hit the road, he gunned it.

"You're not going to..." she gasped as he sank a finger into her, "make me come before we get to my place if you're driving so fast."

He slanted a look at her, brow raised. "Is that a challenge?"

She sucked in a gasp as he began to fingerfuck her with slow, rhythmic plunges of his finger.

"You're going to wreck. This vehicle's huge and the console is so wide you can hardly reach me."

"Scoot closer them and spread your legs farther," was his only response.

"You do have long arms, though," she continued in a shiver of a voice.

He liked the way she was puzzling through what was happening. By the time they hit the turn for the South Market District where her apartment was, she'd be screaming and writhing with her release.

"Get out your phone, *cher*."

"Wh-what?"

He swirled his finger around her clit before plunging it inside her again. "Take out your phone and video what I'm doing to you."

"Oh my God."

"It'll be sexy. You know you'll want to watch it again. Do it."

She fumbled in her purse at her side and came out with her phone. She nestled it between her knees and angled it. As soon as her own pussy and his fingers came onto the screen, she moaned and he nearly jizzed in his jeans. The sight was the fucking hottest thing he'd ever seen.

"Now watch your pussy come for me."

Her breathing changed. Each rasping noise came faster and louder as he alternated between her clit and her soaking wet entrance. She was shaking, vibrating his fingers, hand, arm. God, this woman was so damn hot and working her out of his system wasn't even an option anymore.

But he was a Marine and a Knight and that meant he had a backup plan, which meant he was demanding more from her and damn the consequences. The past two weeks had been hell and debriefing after the drug bust on the shore had only rolled into another damn mission, and the final story was that he'd just returned from some bullshit town in Texas after witnessing shit that no human should ever see.

After dropping off Rocko and his brothers, he'd come straight to the club, determined to find Dahlia and if he didn't see her there, he'd planned to go to her apartment. But her sweet scents of arousal wafting from the passenger seat and the soft, tormenting moans leaving her lips made him forget all the crap he'd lived through since being with her last.

She gripped his wrist, guiding him to fingerfuck her faster. "Ben, I'm so close. Right there, oh God..."

The phone slipped in her grasp, but she righted it as her orgasm hit. On screen, he watched her pussy pulsate even as her juices flooded him. Her cry echoed through the SUV and his balls clenched so hard that he growled.

He continued to run his fingers over her slick heat to the tune of her quivering sighs. When she let the phone drop to the floor and threw her head back with a final rasping cry, a satisfied smile crossed his face.

"You're so full of yourself," she shot out.

Damn, he loved that sass too.

"I think I have good reason to be." He pulled his fingers free of her pussy and brought them to his lips.

"Holy shit." She issued a shaky breath, watching him lick at his fingers. Her flavors were just as he remembered. Better, in fact. Pure, sweet woman.

He pulled up in front of her apartment and cut the engine.

When Dahlia met his gaze, her eyes were hazy with pleasure and the passion that had driven him to hightail it back the minute he was debriefed.

He nodded toward the floor. "You may want to pick up your phone and call your date, let him know you're not going to make it."

* * * * *

They barely made it through the door before Dahlia's skirt was up and Ben's fingers were inside her again. She clung to him, swirling her tongue over his as he worked a magic that had her inner walls screaming for more.

"Fuck, I love the way you kiss me back," he muttered between thrusts of his tongue. When he withdrew, he gazed down at her for several long heartbeats. She swallowed hard at the need chiseled into his rugged features.

"Forgive me for everything I've done, Dahlia."

She didn't reply but he didn't seem to need it— simply asking forgiveness was enough to ease his conscience. He closed the door and locked it and then pinned her to the wood, staring at her until her need spiked again.

"Ben." She had no idea what she was asking for. Her body demanded and her heart was on the verge of begging for more from this man. But her mind was clear.

Well, sort of.

He traced his lips across her jaw, licking at her earlobe with each pass. She was soaking wet and aching for Ben, and there was no way he was staying clothed another second.

She tore off his T-shirt and went for his cargo pants. He moaned against her throat as she ran her fingers over the hard length of his cock curving upward toward his abs. She sagged at the knees, starting to slide down the door to take him in her mouth.

But he caught her elbows. "No, honey. Not this time. Turn around and place your hands over your head."

Holy crap. She was melting into a puddle, couldn't even think straight to obey his command. When she didn't move, he eased her around, took her wrists and locked them to the door.

The bulk of his body against her spine and the way his cock nestled at her behind only inspired uncontrollable need. She twisted her head, panting. "I need this."

"Yes, you do. And I'll give it to you, *cher*. If you promise me there won't be any more dates."

"I... I'm not promising that. I don't owe you anything and —"

She sucked in a gasp as he probed her drenched folds from behind, finding her opening and sinking his fingers in shallowly. She wiggled to make him slide his fingers deeper, but he resisted.

"Right now, we're working out what is happening between us. And we don't want any distractions. Promise me, Dahlia."

If she didn't, he might not continue with his sexual explorations and leave her panting with want.

Besides, she hadn't wanted to date Mike's friend anyhow.

She nodded at the same time she arched her back, pushing her hips up. "I need your fingers."

"Honey, you'll get more than my fingers. Is that a promise?"

"Yes," she said raggedly.

"Good." He painted her juices up and down her slick seam. "Now stay in that position."

The only sound in the apartment was her rough breaths and the rustle of clothing. The sounds heightened her need and by the time he poised his rubber-sheathed cock at her opening, she was gagging for it.

"Spread your legs farther," he demanded.

A noise left her throat as she did his bidding. Arousal dripped down her inner thighs, and she was helpless against his commands. She'd do anything he asked if only he'd end this sweet torment right now and fuck her.

He ran the head of his cock up over her pussy, sinking only enough to stretch her opening with the flared head. In her ear, he whispered, "You want this?"

"I want your cock."

"Oh, you'll have it, little temptress." He pushed inside her. She cried out, curling her fingers against the door for purchase. He wrapped an arm around her middle, anchoring her to his big body and supporting her as he drove inside her. Churning hips, his teeth grazing her throat. She closed her eyes and gave herself over to sensation.

Ben was all she'd wanted for months, and now that she had him, she wasn't going to waste time dwelling on when it would end. She only wanted the high he gave her, the complete ecstasy that made her forget even her own name.

When they came down from their releases, he turned her into his arms and lifted her. Staring into her eyes for a long moment before carrying her to her bed for round two.

Then three.

* * * * *

Dahlia's car was back home—again. For the second time, she'd left with Ben and for the second time, he'd managed to get her vehicle back to her. How?

She hadn't given him her keys and that could only mean that he'd hotwired it. Great—she was sleeping with... obsessed with... a car thief.

Just thinking of Ben gave her an occasional twitch, as if her body still experienced the aftershocks of their blazing night of passion. She clamped her knees together and waited her turn in line at the café for her hazelnut coffee.

She didn't usually make the stop to the coffee shop and brewed her own, but this morning, she wasn't willing to stick around her apartment for another second. Each time she caught a whiff of Ben's lingering aftershave, she wanted to scream and that would likely bring in negative calls from her neighbors.

The man had freakin' left—again. And Dahlia was officially an idiot. There was no other word to describe her actions.

She pushed out a sigh and tapped a heel on the tile floor. The line moved forward, and she shuffled with it.

This was the story of her life. Shuffling along, only getting small glimpses into what her real life could be. She had flashes of amazing highs—like when Ben had pinned her to his vehicle and dragged rough moans from her. Not to mention him licking his fingers clean after—

"What can I get you?"

She opened her mouth to speak, and her phone buzzed.

She froze. She was not answering that. She hadn't given Ben her number, but that didn't mean he didn't have it. The man hadn't had her keys either, yet he'd gotten her car back to her apartment.

She mumbled out her order and was shuffled on down the line while the barista prepared her drink.

Only when she had the cup in hand and was on her way out the door did she check her phone. *Damn. Serena.*

She hadn't explained why she'd skipped out on her blind date.

Juggling her phone and coffee, she started a slow stroll through the neighborhood. Typically, the walk gave her pleasure on her days off. Right now, she wasn't feeling very calm, though.

She put the phone to her ear and took a sip of the creamy hazelnut goodness, the only good thing about her day so far. She braced herself for her friend's irritation.

"Oh, so she isn't dead. She answered her phone."

Okay, irritation was a little understated.

"I'm sorry, Serena. Something came up last night."

"Wasn't that your car I saw in the parking lot?"

Shit. Think fast.

She could feed her friend a line about a sick friend or a call-off at work and a second shift to work, but Serena would see right through the lie.

"Mike and I were really disappointed and so was Mike's friend. He was really looking forward to meeting you. He'd seen you at the wedding."

Fabulous. Hadn't Dahlia had one champagne too many and ended up busting out to the *Electric Slide* near the end?

"I'm sorry."

"That's all you have to say?" Serena asked. A beat of silence and then, "Fine. It's obvious you're sneaking around or seeing someone else. The worst thing about this is that you're not being honest with me and I thought we were friends."

Dahlia groaned. "Look, I ran into an old friend. One thing led to another and — "

"Old friend? Who was it? Because if you're back on that Alexander thing, I'm dumping you as *my* friend. I'm not going to sit back and watch you get involved in that toxic — "

"It's not Alexander." Though it may be just as toxic. Ben was like an addiction she couldn't turn down. "I'm sorry again, Serena. It won't happen again. It's over now."

"Oh. Good! Then you can meet us tonight for drinks. Mike's friend is still in town."

"I can't. I have another obligation. But look, I need to duck into the drugstore for a minute. I'll call you soon." She ended with a false brilliance to her voice that, if Serena was really listening, she'd know was brittle. They ended the call.

Dahlia looked at her surroundings and slurped down her coffee rather than savor it. The quaint shops of this district usually made her feel peaceful, uplifted with the energy of the city. But right now, she was too irritated, not with her friend but herself. Why had she let Ben derail her determination again?

She turned around and headed toward home again. She'd start the day over, beginning by going home and changing her sheets. Washing all her bedding so it didn't smell like Ben was step one to purging the man from her memory.

So, when was she going to stop feeling his touch all over her body? It was as if the man had left behind a ghost touch, and she could feel each callused stroke of his fingertips.

She made it back to her apartment and had barely dropped her empty cup in the trash when her cell rang.

"Kyle." She held her breath, waiting for him to call her in to work on her day off.

"I warned you about personal calls, Dahlia."

"What? I'm not even working today."

"I know. And some guy named Ben keeps calling demanding he speak with you."

Oh God. He was going to get her fired.

He's trying to contact me.

Heart thumping, she stared into space, seeing nothing but the man's chiseled jaw as he lowered his head to kiss her.

She had to put a stop to this before he jeopardized her livelihood and she ended up broke and living with her father again. No way could she be under his radar again.

"I don't know any Ben."

"Hmm. That isn't what he's saying."

Dammit, she was going to have to hunt down the gorgeous man and wring his neck. Only she'd end up on her knees with his thick, deliciously veined cock in her mouth.

Shut off your libido.

"Turn him over to the police for making false 911 calls," she suggested.

"I did. I just wanted to let you know so you can warn this Ben guy before the police pay him a visit."

Dropping her head back, she exhaled slowly and tried to come up with some way to respond to her boss. This whole day was really sucking so far. The only good thing about it was she wouldn't need to take an Uber to pick up her car at the club.

"Fine, Kyle. Thanks for the head's up." With that, she ended the call. Two seconds didn't pass before her door buzzer rang.

"Fucking hell," she murmured and went to press the button on the wall to answer. She didn't even get to speak before Ben's voice filled her space.

"Dahlia, it's me."

Her eyes flew open wide as she stared at the speaker as if the man had materialized there.

"Can I come up?" he asked.

Panic set in. She hadn't stripped the sheets off her bed yet. It was a little rumpled but they could still fall into it. Wait—what was she thinking? She wasn't having sex with Ben again, wasn't even going to go downstairs to look at his face. If she did, she'd be a goner, lost in the green pools of his eyes and jonesing for all that muscle.

"No, you can't come up."

Good, she prided herself. She'd managed to keep an even tone.

"Dahlia, I'm sorry. Something came up and I had to make an emergency run."

"Is this for your job?" she heard herself ask. This was ridiculous. Holding a conversation through the intercom was even dumber than getting into his SUV and videoing him fingering her pussy the previous night.

A trickle of warmth slid through her lower abdomen and pooled between her thighs. She still had the video on her phone, but she could have the real thing. All she had to do was unlock the door and let him in.

"Yes, my job. Something came up," he said.

Anger swept her. "I thought you were in construction. Or demolition. Why are you getting calls in the middle of the night? I think you're a car thief." In the back of her mind, she was ignoring that cocky swagger that reminded her of all the Marines her daddy had paraded through their home over the years.

"What?"

"You're pretty capable of getting my car back to me without even a set of keys. Look, I don't want anything to do with you, Ben. We had a few nights of fun, but it's finished."

There—she'd said it.

Ouch.

Her gut instinct was to take it back, hit the button to unlock the door and let him come in and fuck her brains out.

All day.

It was her day off, after all.

No. She had to get a grip. Not even a man who could use his cock like Ben could was worth all this drama let alone the feelings of letdown each time she woke to find him gone.

"I'm not a car thief, *cher*. Just let me come up and we can talk."

"No."

"Then come down and I'll take you out."

"Not a chance." She could only imagine the things he'd do to her on the street, with all those alleys to hide in.

He pushed out a breath, and she could nearly see him running his hand through his hair. "Fine. Then meet me tonight and let me make it up to you."

"I have a date tonight."

Was that a groan she heard cut off by the intercom?

"Dammit. You promised."

"You promised you were staying till morning how many times now? I'm finished with promises too."

A second passed, and then his voice came to her clearly. "Fuck, I'm getting a text from my brother that the cops are looking for me concerning a fake 911 call?"

She couldn't stop a giggle, but luckily, he didn't hear it.

"Dahlia, open the door. There's too much between us."

That she heard loud and clear. Time to cut ties and be the strong, independent woman her daddy had raised her to be.

She pressed the button and leaned close to the speaker, trying not to think of his lips next to her ear. "I can't see you tonight or any night, Ben. Please forget this address."

* * * * *

Ben didn't think he could be in a fouler mood. Running on no sleep, the woman he couldn't quit thinking about had dumped him, the cops were on his ass about making fake 911 calls, and he was on orders to show up at a fucking barbecue for Colonel Jackson at eighteen hundred hours.

Or risk being court martialed.

And now his brothers were relating a story about his little sister that was threatening the enamel of his teeth as he viciously ground them.

He glanced in the rearview at Dylan, who was speaking. "The guy was trying to take advantage of Lexi."

Ben growled. "Let me get this straight. Some asshole came into the flower shop where Lexi works and tried to schmooze money from her."

Dylan gave a solemn nod. The rest of the Knights were grim-faced, and even Rocko appeared to be bothered by the story. Ben gripped the steering wheel hard, wishing the cracking of his joints was this motherfucker's bones.

"Start at the beginning," Ben ordered.

"I guess Lexi's been seeing this guy on the down-low," Dylan said.

"And you know this from Lexi herself?"

"No, from Tyler."

Lexi's twin counterpart would know. The two were like one and the same person, equally as beautiful and drawing male attention since they were thirteen and Ben and their brothers had started beating the boys back. Only Tyler was savvy in the ways of the world while Lexi was too sweet to be anything but sucked in.

"Fuck," Ben bit off.

"What's the big deal about your sister seeing some guy?" Rocko asked. All five Knights turned their glares on him. To his credit, the SEAL did not flinch, just shrugged. "Well?"

"Lexi suffered a lack of oxygen when she was born. She's not handicapped, but she's... special. She's perfectly capable of dealing with anything life throws her way, unless it has to do with numbers." Ben waited for Rocko to catch on. When he didn't, he said, "She can't deal with numbers, and that includes money."

"Ohhh. Fuck," Rocko said softly.

"Yeah, she's smart as a whip when it comes to literature. Quotes things that none of us can understand the meaning of and she's sporty as hell. Lexi can even outrun Ben here." Dylan waved at him.

"I wouldn't go that far," Ben grumbled. "Though she's damn fast. So, what did this asshole do to try to get money from her? He must have known her weakness." Just saying that pissed Ben off. Nobody fucked with his family, let alone Lexi. Each Knight protected her like the Templars protected the Grail.

"Tyler says Lexi was dating him. She must have gotten close enough to the jackass to tell him about herself."

"Dammit," three of the brothers said together.

"Okay, I'm lost again," Rocko spoke up. "Tyler is...?"

"Lexi's twin."

"Another Knight brother? How many of you assholes *are* there?"

Ben shot him a glare over his shoulder. "Tyler's female. And watch your mouth."

Rocko was nonplussed. "There has to be a story behind Tyler having a boy's name."

"Yeah, she was a surprise twin. Our parents didn't know she was coming then out she came, and since they had so many boys, they never expected one girl let alone two. Our mother had always loved the name Lexi, so she got the one and only female name they'd picked out."

"And Tyler got the leftovers." Rocko bobbed his head as he put it all together.

"I'm so kicking your ass," Ben warned.

"Save it for this guy who tried to get into Lexi's bank account," Sean said from the passenger seat.

"Fine. We'll get through this mandatory barbecue of the colonel's and then tonight we'll go look up Lexi's 'boyfriend,' shall we?" Ben took the final turn that would take them to the private road leading to Colonel Jackson's home.

"Why are we invited to a barbecue again?" Sean drawled as they were swallowed by a grove of trees on either side of the road old enough to have been planted when Louisiana was founded.

"I don't for a minute believe it's for the food," Ben said.

"You think he's sending us somewhere?" Chaz spoke up from the back.

Ben didn't respond as the house came into view. Not any house, but one of those big old Southern homes that seemed to sprawl across acres, with big front windows and columns that had probably kept the place standing during some battle of the Civil War.

Sean whistled. "Guess it pays to be a high-ranking officer."

After parking and cutting the engine, Knight Ops piled out of the vehicle and fell in behind Ben. As the natural leader, he led them to the double doors. Using the doorbell irritated him, though. It roused bad memories of earlier that day when Dahlia had not only told him she wasn't seeing him but that he should forget her address.

Pressing his lips into a firm line, he waited for a butler to answer the door, but it was Jackson himself. Out of uniform, he might be any guy at a country club. In summer slacks and a polo shirt, he could even be a golfer. Ben should be golfing right now, and instead he was neck-deep in special ops that so far had sent them on some bullshit missions. Knowing what he did of Jackson, though, he figured those operations were just warmups.

Ben saluted his superior officer, as did the rest of the team.

"At ease, Marines. This is a party and I see none of you dressed for it." He glanced over their cargo pants, combat boots and black T-shirts. "At least leave the weapons at the door."

They stepped into the grand foyer and it was easy to see some belle sweeping down that curving staircase in a big dress. Sean let out another low whistle.

Jackson was waiting for them to check their weapons, but nobody was willing to make the first move. Ben reached for his sidearm and set it on a table next to a huge vase of fresh-cut flowers most likely from some extravagant Southern garden it took two gardeners to keep up.

One by one, the guys disarmed and when Jackson was satisfied, the tough old fucker actually smiled. He took off through the entryway. "Party's out back on the lanai."

Ben had been in a lot of odd situations, and this was gaining a top spot on that list. In his position, he'd pow-wowed with a lot of higher ranking officers, but why they were invited to a barbecue at the colonel's personal residence was weird as fuck.

Outside, the fragrance of grilled meats hit them, and Jackson gestured to a metal tub of beer on ice. "Help yourselves, boys."

"Now this is turning out to be a real nice party," Sean drawled as he moved off toward a small group of women sitting by the pool. Any bikini had a Knight's head turning, and typically Ben was no different. But not today, not with Dahlia's scent still filling his mind and the silky feel of her sliding down over his cock fresh in his memory.

Jackson let the Knights and Rocko mill with the guests at their leisure as he stood talking and joking with some other old gentlemen.

"I don't know a fucking person here, do you?" Dylan asked.

"Nope." Ben tipped the beer to his lips. "Just see where this thing goes. And don't hack Jackson's computer."

Dylan cocked a brow. "I'm insulted that you'd think I'd do that. I wouldn't bother with the computers. If I was hacking anything, it would be the security code to Jackson's gun safe."

* * * * *

Dahlia descended the stairs and stopped dead when she reached the bottom. She stared at the weapons piled on the entry table. "What the...?" Her daddy threw some weird parties in his time, but she'd never seen this. Typically, his guests were old friends and family members, especially when it came to his birthday barbecues.

She took a second to glance in the mirror at her appearance. Her eyes weren't red or swollen—a good thing. She'd gone upstairs to shed a few tears, which wasn't like her at all, and her daddy would pick up on that like a flea on a dog.

She was just so out of sorts today, and she didn't feel like mingling with guests at all, though she didn't have any choice but to slap a smile in place and party like her father was turning fifty-nine.

Pausing at the lanai, she smoothed her hands over her long black sundress. Her sandals made a soft clicking noise as she crossed the patio and stopped dead at the sight of the Marine at the bar. That back, the broad shoulders, were so familiar that her heart somersaulted.

But something about the man wasn't quite right. She watched him as he turned into profile, and relief swept her. That wasn't Ben at all. Besides, why would he be here when...

Hold on.

There wasn't just one Marine here but six, by her weapons count in the foyer. She scanned the group of guests, drinking, laughing, talking, even swimming. And standing in groups, sticking out like aliens at a Fourth of July parade, were men dressed in black T-shirts and cargo pants. Two of them had the same way of holding their shoulders that Ben did. And—

"What the hell are you doing here?" The gritty voice speared her as Ben's lips were suddenly at her ear.

She whirled to face him, and God, did he look amazing as a Marine.

On the heels of that thought was something along the lines of *fuck, he's a Marine*.

She should have guessed that her father had some hand in this. Leave it to him to meddle in her love life.

Without waiting for Ben to say more, she grabbed his arm and hauled him several feet away from the nearest group that could overhear their conversation.

In a low urgent tone, she said, "Did you tell my father about us?"

He blinked down at her. All she wanted was to throw her arms around him and slide her thigh up his hip, tilting her pussy toward that thick cock she craved so bad.

"Your father?" A stunned expression crossed his rugged features. "Jackson's your *father*?"

"You didn't know that?"

"Hell no. How could I? No last names, remember?" He narrowed his eyes at her. "Did you know my position?"

"Well, now I'm guessing that you're the new OFFSUS team, but I'm not supposed to know anything about that. But no, I did not know when I met you in the club."

"Shit."

"Shit is right. I need a drink." She took off for the bar, leaving Ben behind her, though she could feel his hot gaze burning into her back. She picked up a wine glass as he reached her side again.

Hovering over her, he said, "You look fucking stunning in that dress. I want to rip it off you, Dahlia."

Her insides melted but she took a sip of the wine to cover her reaction. The only way to deal with this man—and keep herself from fucking him in the pool house—was to find some semblance of cool. Though that was difficult when the real problem struck her.

She was screwing around with a member of a special ops team that was put into danger daily. Something she never wanted for herself.

All her life, she'd watched her mother struggle with worry over where her husband was and if he'd ever come home. Dahlia had never gotten over the idea that constant stress had taken her mother in the end and the cancer had just been the final blow.

She sipped her wine and tried not to reveal any of this on her face, but Ben was looking at her too closely.

"Were you crying?"

"What? Of course not." She buried her nose in her glass again, inhaling the fruity notes of the Zinfandel.

He wrapped his fingers around hers holding the glass and stared down into what felt like her soul. "You're not throwing me away so easily. I—"

"Dahlia, dear, could you come here for a moment? I'd like you to meet someone." Her father's raised voice ripped through whatever sexual wall wouldn't crumble between her and Ben.

"Excuse me." She relinquished her wine glass to him and walked away to join her father. He held out an arm and slid it around her shoulders as she stopped before another Marine. Though he wasn't dressed like the others in attendance, there was no doubt in Dahlia's mind of what he was.

"Dahlia, this is John Winters. I've told you about him."

She extended a hand, fighting the tremors she still felt after being in Ben's presence. As she accepted the man's firm handshake, she swore a growl came from somewhere behind them.

"Yes, my father speaks highly of you."

Winters squeezed her hand a moment too long. He had a nice smile. A direct, straightforward gaze. There was no nonsense about this man. She wouldn't be left wondering if he was a car thief and discovering he was just a member of OFFSUS.

Ha! Just a member of OFFSUS.

"Why don't you two get better acquainted? I see Charles flagging me down," her father said, leaving them alone.

From the corner of her eye, she spotted Ben angling their way as if to break them up, but her father intercepted and sent him off in another direction, probably on some errand. The fact that her daddy didn't want her involved with a Marine like Ben but was matchmaking her to Winters had her swinging on a pendulum of confusion.

On one hand, her inner rebel child wanted to make a beeline right for Ben and to hell with her father's thinking on the matter. But she wasn't into scary missions and not knowing where her lover was or if he was even alive either. She'd sworn off that life long ago and most likely, Winters was in a very cushy position.

Not that she was looking for a boyfriend in either man. She was just fine flying solo.

While Winters spoke to her about the party and the weather, Ben came at her again. Once more he was blocked by her daddy. He made two more failed attempts before dinner was served. And when they sat down to dine, she was placed between her father and Winters, leaving Ben scowling from halfway down the table.

She didn't dare look his direction. The heat coming off the man was enough to turn her on from ten feet away, and her body was not about to let her forget whose touch had done those unspeakable things to her hours ago.

Chapter Five

"A word, Captain Knight." Jackson held open the door for him to pass into the house.

Here it comes.

At this point, Ben would welcome a dangerous mission. Hell, he'd go after ISIS singlehandedly rather than watch Jackson matchmake Dahlia with that desk dog Winters.

He ground his teeth and gave a nod as he passed into the house. Jackson closed the door and turned to face Ben. Their gazes locked.

"Have you been fucking my little girl?"

He might have choked on his tongue if his jaw hadn't been clenched so tight. "Sir?"

"You heard me. Don't give me that stupid act, either. I can see you sniffing around her."

Ben didn't have anything to say, so he stood stiffly, waiting for the bomb to drop, sure Jackson was shipping him off to Antarctica just to keep him away from Dahlia.

"Sir, I had no idea Dahlia would be here. I only came because of your order."

"And Dahlia didn't mention it?"

"I didn't even know she was your daughter. She told me she had a date."

At that, Jackson chuckled. "She does. A standing date every year on this day, with me for my birthday."

It had to be done. Ben had to say what was on his mind.

"If I may ask, sir, what are your intentions with Winters regarding your daughter?"

His eyes sharpened. "That is none of your business, Captain. Now get out there and gather your men. The party is officially over for you."

"Sir." He saluted and went back outside. He did gather his men, but he had no intention of leaving.

"Uh-oh. I see that look. I *like* that look. What's going on?" Sean rubbed his palms together like a child eager for ice cream.

He led them to the foyer, and each of them took his sidearm again. Ben leaned in. "We're not leaving yet. That woman whose car you collected from the club for me? That's Jackson's daughter's."

Jaws dropped but amusement quickly replaced shock. Dylan grinned. "You're screwing around with Jackson's daughter?"

"I didn't know it until today. But yeah. He is guarding her heavily, and I need to speak with her."

"Say no more. We'll bring her to you outside. Operation kidnap the colonel's daughter is underway." Sean waved toward the two exits, and the men broke off with Sean in command.

* * * * *

Dahlia came out of the powder room and gave a small cry as a wall of muscle clad in black cotton encircled her.

"What's going on? Are we under siege?" At this point, she'd expect anything. She looked from man to man, her heart rate spiking. But not one of them was Ben.

"What is this?" She straightened her shoulders and met their gazes one by one. Judging by their appearance, several were his brothers, and all of them were doing his bidding.

"Our captain requests an audience, miss."

Captain? Dear God. He's not only in OFFSUS, but he's leading the team.

The man speaking was almost as tall as Ben, with the same dark hair and his eyes were a warm green with gold flecks, but his jaw wasn't as angled. Or maybe it was the playful tilt to his lips that set him apart from Ben.

"Come with us." This guy could also be Ben's brother. She swore his eyes were sparkling the same way.

She shook her head. "I'm not going anywhere with you. And I'm not talking to Ben."

They just stared at her. Finally, one spoke up. "We have orders to pick you up and carry you if necessary, miss."

She balled her fist. She wanted to punch something, but any attempts made on these hard bodies would only end with her wearing a cast. She closed her eyes and started counting.

"I don't think she's willing to come with us, Sean."

"Doesn't look that way." The guy who must be Sean sighed. "I guess we just pick her up then." When he started moving toward her, she threw up her hands.

"No! You're not carrying me anywhere, and I'm not speaking to your captain." Looking for an exit between the broad torsos barring her way was futile. She could barely see gaps of air between them. These Marines knew how to impersonate a cement block wall.

"We have our orders, miss," one insisted.

"Fine! I'll go." That didn't mean she had to listen to anything Ben said, and she definitely was not letting him touch her.

One kiss, her body said.

She mentally slapped herself and waited for the men to move. They walked out of the house with her between them as if she was going to make a break for it. Not that she wasn't considering it, but now that she knew what type of work Ben did, she realized he'd be able to hunt her down and get her alone any time he wanted. At least if she spoke to him on her father's property, chances were things wouldn't get out of hand.

Who was she kidding? Ben could have her panties off and flung in the nearest shrubbery with a single flash of his eyes.

When the two men in front of her stopped walking, she nearly barreled into their backs. She skidded to a stop and the men flanking her on either side and behind her did as well.

The line of bodies broke and Ben shouldered his way in. A single nod from him had them all scattering, leaving Dahlia standing there with Ben— alone.

She let her gaze skitter away.

"I don't blame you for being angry with me. I should have told you what I do for a living. But it's classified information. I'm sure you understand that with a colonel for a father."

"Oh yeah, I do." The words tasted like acid on her tongue. Having a colonel for a father was one thing. She'd also grown up and moved out, which had eliminated some of the constant worry and stress of him being in that role. But she couldn't do that with Ben, not if she let him into her life.

Which she wasn't. Couldn't.

He was staring at her, and her eyes betrayed her. A single peek of his burning expression had her weak in the knees.

"Dahlia," he said softly, stepping forward and skimming his knuckles along her cheekbone, "can you forgive me?"

She wanted to lean into his touch like a stray kitten starved for affection, but she slapped his hand away. "There's nothing to forgive. We're nothing to each other."

Lines appeared around each of his eyes. "Is that true? You don't feel anything when you look at me? You feel nothing in my bed? Don't tell me that you weren't burning up for me each and every time I sucked your nipples or ran my fingers over your clit or plunged my cock—"

Her weak knees were threatening collapse. "That's enough, Ben. Please, just stop trying to get me in your bed again. Things won't work out between us. Not ever."

Something crossed his face, and oh, how she wanted to examine that look further, but that meant falling harder for him.

"I felt horrible leaving your bed those times without explaining why. I should have broken the rules and told you. Especially after you told me about your job. It was the perfect opportunity."

She set a hand on her hip and cocked it. "About that. You called my work looking for me and that got me in trouble."

"I'll smooth it out with your boss."

"No, you will not. You'll stay away from my workplace and you won't call there again."

He arched a brow in that bad-boy way that had her nipples bunching into tight knots. "What if I get into a car accident and need rescued?"

"Not even then."

"If I'm trapped in the twisted metal and need the jaws of life."

"Nope. Because I'm sure you can get yourself out, knowing what I know about you now."

He moved closer, bringing his spicy, earthy scent with him. And God, he filled out black cotton like a... well, a Marine.

She breathed shallowly to keep herself from being overcome by manly, masculine... maleness, for lack of a better way of putting it.

"What if I've already wrecked, Dahlia? If I've careened out of control over a woman."

Her heart skipped.

He lowered his head and used his knuckles under her chin to draw her face upward. "You're driving me crazy, *cher*. I need to touch you."

She ordered her brain to make her shake her head, but it never happened. In fact, she tipped her head up and closed her eyes.

"So beautiful," he said faintly, warm breath washing over her lips. He traced a path down her jaw to thumb her lower lip. Juices flooded her panties, and she was ready to dive into the bushes with this

108

man and to hell with Winters or her daddy and anybody else looking on. She wanted Ben.

"There's so much more I want to know about you. I *will* know. As soon as I get back."

Her eyes flew open. "What?"

He flexed his jaw, causing the tendon in the crease to flicker. "Your father's sending us on another mission. We fly out tonight."

She swallowed the hard lump that had suddenly risen in her throat. "I can't do this, Ben. I can't be with a man like you."

He swooped in and claimed her lips, wiping her words off her tongue with a flick of his own. With a hand planted on her lower back and one on her nape, he drew her into his kiss, tormenting her for five heartbeats before drawing back.

She searched his face. Dammit, no matter how much distance she wanted to put between them, it was too late. He'd wormed his way close to her heart after only a few meetings, and she would never stop thinking about him if she didn't give it at least a small chance.

"I'm sorry, honey. It's my job. But I'm asking you to wait for me. When I come back, we'll spend time together. Go away maybe."

"Don't make promises you can't keep. You can't even stay a whole night with me, so how are we leaving town together?"

His chest heaved as if he struggled with the idea. Finally, he nodded. "You're right. I can't make those promises. But know that I want to. Will you wait for me, Dahlia?"

Her mind might be screaming to run the other direction, but there was too much chemistry between them to be simple lust, and she'd always wonder what could have been with Ben.

"Do I at least get to know your last name?"

The corner of his lips flashed upward. "Knight. It's Knight."

"Well, Ben Bartholomew Knight, I guess I'll see you when you return."

She got an even bigger crooked smile, but it faded as quickly as it had come. He ran his thumb over her lower lip again as his gaze intensified. "Wait for me. And don't see that asshole Winters in the meantime."

* * * * *

"Get your ass on that chopper, Captain, before it takes off without you."

The order came through Ben's coms device and into his ear, but he recognized Colonel Jackson's voice. He glanced around the airfield for the man but didn't see him. He was probably happily sitting inside the hangar, sipping a Dewars and laughing his ass off at how he'd managed to get rid of his daughter's love interest.

Chaz and Roades were waving at him from the chopper, and putting his head down against the wind generated by the propellers, he strode to the waiting aircraft.

He slipped in and someone shut the door. Seconds later, they lifted off. Knight Ops stared at him.

"Just coming from my brothers, this is bad enough, but Rocko is even glaring at me. I didn't get us into this situation. You were all gung-ho to be in OFFSUS when asked."

"We didn't even have twelve hours between missions to sink our dicks into something soft and wet," Chaz said.

Agreement sounded among them.

"It's not my fault you can't find a willing woman. But I am not the reason we're leaving the country tonight."

They looked at him as if to ask, *Isn't it?*

"You're sleeping with the colonel's daughter, so he's punishing us," Sean said.

"No. He's assigning us a mission and it is our duty to achieve it. Now quit whining about your pricks and buck up, assholes. We need to plan. Who's got the maps?" He looked around the group.

Dylan patted his vest pocket. Each of them were strapped with ammunition, armed to the teeth with everything they needed to drop into a situation, ready to improvise. But he didn't like the morale in the chopper right now.

"Look, I'll buy you each a hotel room and a hooker for a weekend when we return. Okay?"

That got a few smiles. Rocko's teeth flashed white in the camo paint of his face. Someday that smile was going to get him sniped. "I can get my own women."

"Yeah? You exclusive with someone?" Ben thought asking about mundane life things might ease some of the tension shooting his way.

"Yeah, her name's Jenna. And Karly. Gabriella is might pretty too."

They all laughed, and the release was just what they needed.

He gestured to Dylan. "Give me the maps."

Sean reached into his vest and pulled out his cell.

Ben looked up, pinning him in his stare. "You know we aren't allowed cells." If they were captured, it was too easy to find out their identities.

"I'm just checking on Lexi."

Damn, Ben had almost forgotten about their issue with Lexi's "boyfriend" trying to wipe out her bank account. The man would have to wait for their return to have his legs broken.

He slapped the cell from his brother's hand. "We're in the air, man. It will mess with the instruments. We'll deal with the guy when we get back."

"And what about that Winters dude?" Rocko asked.

Ben's head whipped his way. "What about him?"

"You looked like you wanted to knock out a few of his teeth too, when he was talking to your lady."

He wasn't even going to deny Dahlia was his. As far as he was concerned, she was.

"Did you tell her we'll be gone two weeks minimum?" Rocko cocked a brow.

He shook his head. "She'll find out soon enough."

In fact, she'd most likely forget about agreeing to wait for him. Why would she anyway? She deserved better than a half-ass, part-time relationship with a man who could be killed in the line of duty at any moment. Dammit, why had he asked her to wait? He shouldn't have put that yoke on her to bear.

For a second, he considered texting her with Sean's phone and to hell with the chopper's instruments. But he placed it under his boot. With one hard stomp, the phone shattered, all communication with the outside world lost. Whatever happened with Lexi or Dahlia would have to wait until the mission was complete.

Hopefully Ben had someone to come back and explain to.

* * * * *

"Princess. I didn't expect you." Dahlia's father leaned in to kiss her cheek and welcome her into the

113

house. She stepped inside the grand entry, casting a look at the sideboard where the guns had been last.

"Hi, Dad. I wondered if we can talk about something."

"Sure. My office or the living room? I can fix some mimosas."

She shook her head. "The office is fine."

He arched a brow at her but didn't ask her reasons for the formal visit. They walked to the office and he closed the door behind them. Turning to her, he said, "I'm not sure what to expect from you, Dahlia."

"Sit down, Dad. I just want to ask you some things."

"I hope this isn't about life. After your mother passed, I never could quite get a handle on how to raise a daughter."

"You did fine, Daddy." She offered him a soft smile, the mention of her late mother making her yearn for understanding.

She folded her hands and waited for her father to sink into his big leather chair. She studied his lined face, wondering how much of those had been put there by his own missions and worrying about the men he led.

"You're making me nervous, honey."

She nodded and tried to focus what she wanted to say. "I'd like to know more about Operation Freedom Flag."

He was still for a long minute and then sat back in his chair. "You know that's classified information, princess."

"Yes, but I've never asked before. Because it was never important before."

He narrowed his eyes, but she caught a hint of resignation in them. "Is this about Knight?"

"Yes."

"Damn. I knew he was screwing around with you."

"Dad!"

"Look, you don't want a Marine for a mate, and you definitely do not want *that* Marine."

Like all contrary daughters, she squared her shoulders. "Why not?"

"He's not for you. You need someone steady."

"And in the country?" Her prompt didn't even get a change of expression out of her father. The man could do a snow job on Santa Claus after he read her father's name on the naughty list.

"Dahlia, I can't tell you where the team is right now."

She looked down at her fingers, inspecting the curves of her nails. "Would you tell me if he's safe, Daddy?"

He pushed out a heavy sigh and pivoted to look out the window. He didn't often show his age, but

115

right now, his face seemed to droop with what she was asking him to disclose.

Finally, he nodded. "As far as we know, they're safe."

"All of them?" she asked.

"All of them." He looked back to her and spread his hands. "Won't you at least consider Winters? He's a good man."

"I'm sure he is, but..." She met her father's gaze. "You know how Mom felt about you?"

"Goddammit."

"Exactly. Goddammit."

They sat in silence, bonded by something she wasn't willing to explain more and he wasn't willing to discuss.

"How long before he returns?" she asked.

"A few more days, we expect. I shouldn't even be telling you that much."

"But you did, and I'm grateful, Daddy. Thank you." She got up and circled the desk as her father stood, reaching out to accept her into his embrace. With her cheek pressed to his uniform shirt, she knew what her mother must have felt each time her father left. She still wasn't convinced the lifestyle was for her, but then again, Ben wasn't asking for more, was he? He only wanted to see her when he returned.

Going on tiptoe, she planted a kiss to her father's leathery cheek. "Thank you."

"Well, don't get used to it."

She smiled as she pulled free of his hold. "I won't." At least for the moment, her heart was at peace. Ben was alive and would be home soon.

* * * * *

Dahlia dropped her huge tote bag containing her knitting to the floor and kicked it under her desk. Joanie eyed her, and Dahlia sighed. "I know, I know. I need to just end it."

The older woman gave her a gentle smile that said she might know Dahlia was referring to more than the project. She hadn't heard from Ben in three and a half weeks. And when she demanded that her father tell her something more, he'd only given her that look. The same one he'd given her when she was little, basically telling her that she wasn't wearing the right uniform to be given that information.

Of course, she was older and refused to be sent away quietly this time. Fat lot of good that did. She'd wheedled and demanded but her father, hard ass that he was, had only given her his usual cold stare and changed the subject.

She hadn't liked the new topic either, since it was about Winters and how the man had been asking about her each time he saw her daddy.

She plopped into her seat and with another heavy sigh, placed her headset on. Luckily, it didn't take long for the calls to come in and distract her. She received a call about a fishing boat accident followed by one from an elderly lady who said someone was trying to break in, but once the authorities arrived on the scene, they found it was a loose board on her house rattling in the wind.

Then the afternoon shift slowed to a crawl and Dahlia added six more inches to her blanket before Joanie came to lean against her desk.

"Honey, if you don't tie that thing off, you'll never get it out the door to take home. Why don't you start something new? I have some pretty blue yarn to share with you."

She glanced down at the thick wad of knitting under her desk, taking up all the knee space. "I guess you're right."

"I get the feeling you're holding on to something else."

"Absolutely not. This... blanket... is stress relief and something to keep me busy between calls. Same as you and Bill and even Kyle over there." She waved toward her boss, who was clacking away with the needles on an ugly green yarn she hoped wasn't a sweater vest, but it probably was.

Joanie's eyes crinkled when she smiled but her lips crinkled when she frowned. Right now, she was frowning at Dahlia. "Sweetie, this job can get to you, but you can't let it. You have to leave things at the door."

"I know. I try."

"Why don't you sneak to the break area and give one of your girlfriends a call? Meet for drinks?"

She sighed again. "Serena's upset with me and Rachel is busy tracking her ovulation so she and Kip can make babies. I haven't heard from my other two friends since their honeymoons. I guess that means they weren't really great friends to begin with."

Joanie patted her arm. "Friends are difficult to keep up with when we're all so busy running separate directions. What about dating?"

Dahlia stiffened in her seat. "I thought I was seeing someone. Well, sort of. He asked me to wait for him while he was away for work, but it's been nearly a month and I haven't heard from him." The fact that she was confiding in this older coworker spoke of how desperately she needed to discuss the matter.

Having the unbiased opinion was golden, though.

"Is it usual for him to get tied up this way for work?"

Dahlia nodded, looking down at her hands.

"Is he worth waiting for?"

Now, *that* she wasn't quite so decided on. She and Ben hadn't made any commitments, only had a good time. Sure, they hit it off and she enjoyed everything from his body to his humor.

But she didn't like his career or the roller coaster he kept strapping her onto.

"It seems like you have some thinking to do," Joanie said as Dahlia received another call.

Putting on her calmest tone, she responded. A woman screamed her panic and Dahlia's adrenaline kicked in. Within seconds, she hunched tensely over her desk, knitting squashed under her boot and Ben the furthest thing from her mind as she walked a caller through performing rescue breathing on her husband.

During these times, Dahlia had a habit of counting down the seconds before the medics arrived. Numbers seemed to flash behind her eyes as she told the woman to once again listen for her husband's breathing.

"H-he's breathing! It's light but I feel it on my cheek!" the caller cried.

Tears hit the backs of Dahlia's eyes. The emotional storm inside her called for a visit to the club, to Ben Knight's bed... But she didn't know when or if she'd ever see him again.

Seconds later, the medics arrived and took over. Dahlia slouched in her chair as relief left her as wrung out as an old dishrag.

"All right, dear?" Joanie asked, seated with her knitting in her lap again. "That was a tough call."

"Yes," she managed to say, because her mind was going a hundred miles a minute. Joanie had asked if Ben was worth waiting for, and she hadn't known how to reply. After that last call, she had a bit more perspective on life.

Just as she was determined to help the people who needed her at the worst possible times of their lives, Ben was out there doing the same—protecting the lives of citizens. And he was no less passionate about it.

She stepped up to Joanie and rested her hand on the woman's shoulder. "I don't know him well enough to say if he is worth waiting for, but I guess I owe it to myself to find out. Thanks for listening to me."

She hurried to the break area and found her phone in her purse. After her father had refused to tell her anything about Ben or his whereabouts, she'd done some digging on her own. It wasn't hard to find a whole family of Marines named Knight. She'd saved a phone number, and now it was time to make the call.

As she leaned against the break table, she tried to slow her heart. The phone rang twice. Halfway through the third, a woman answered.

"Hello, I'm looking for Ben Knight."

"He's not home right now."

"Um... Well, do you know when he may return?"

Was this Ben's mother? The woman sounded too young. Perhaps a sibling.

"I'm not sure of that. Ben is known for going his separate way and coming back with stories about being shacked up with some woman in Miami or Cabo for a weekend."

The words punched Dahlia squarely in the gut. She leaned forward, trying to wrap her head around it.

"Are you one of his girlfriends? I can take a message for him, but I can't guarantee he will get back to you." The woman's accent was deep South. And her sweet drawl was slicing Dahlia to the heart.

"I-I... No, not his girlfriend. No message."

She ended the call and pressed the phone to her chest. Dammit, how stupid could she be? Even if Ben was actually still on some dangerous mission to protect their freedoms, he was a player. Just as she'd suspected early on. But his honeyed request for her to wait for him had been playing around her brain far too many weeks, until she'd forgotten that part of her hesitation.

He was probably just in some tropical climate, sleeping off a sex-a-thon with some gorgeous woman while Dahlia stupidly wasted her thoughts on him. Clinging to a man was not her way, and she was going to break the bad habit starting now.

She deleted the number she'd just called and returned to work. After she took a seat and had her headset at the ready, she reached under her desk, grabbed her knitting and tied it off. The snip of the scissors made Joanie look up and smile at her, but Dahlia wasn't feeling so positive about the break. She needed a little more time to get Captain Ben Knight out of her system.

* * * * *

Ben's skin burned where they'd taken a flame to him. The smell of burning hair had haunted him for days after, even though the hairs on his forearms were long since shriveled and the burns treated.

Fuck, things hadn't just gone sideways—he and his team had dropped straight into the pits of hell when they'd walked into the South American hovel to rescue a US special ops force being held hostage. Then Ben had become the hostage.

He leaned forward and dropped his head into his hands as memories swept him.

Rocko had taken the first bullet, followed by Roades. Dammit, Ben couldn't quit thinking about the pain twisting his little brother's face as he fell. Yet his other brothers kept assuring him Roades was fine, a superficial wound that was on the mend and he was already back to being his usual, snide asshole self.

Ben watched the memory play like a movie again through his head, thinking that at some point his baby brother had grown up and become a true credit to the team he served—he hadn't even made a noise when the bullet had ripped through his leg.

The moment had shocked Ben so much that he hadn't noticed the guy coming up behind him. In seconds, he'd been fighting for his life, a wire around

123

his neck as he was dragged away. To his relief, he hadn't been strangled, but that was short-lived because they'd placed him with the other hostages and added him to the ranks of the tortured.

What he knew of the rest of the mission was cloudy, given in bits and pieces by his brothers. Sean had taken charge, managed to kill a few of the thugs guarding the place and scrambled to get Knight Ops out.

But it was too late to get them all out and he'd had to make the hard decision of saving five and leaving Ben behind. He kept telling Ben that he knew as captain, Ben would have done the same, and that was the only way he'd managed to walk away. Ben knew by that speech that his brother was still aching over being forced into making the choice.

He rubbed at the bandage covering his forearm. He was told to stay out of the sun while the burns healed, but the warm rays were the only thing he had right now. Even thoughts of Dahlia made his stomach roll.

Dear God. Dahlia.

Though she couldn't know it, she was the only thing that had gotten him through that hell. When the enemy came for him to deliver that final beating, Dahlia's beautiful face had given him the strength to break the guard's neck and then turn his own weapon against him.

Sure, four US hostages had gotten to escape, but not before two others were killed. At least Ben had the satisfaction that he'd sent the bad guys on their way to hell and maimed several others who had kept them imprisoned and taken hourly joy in torturing fellow countrymen.

Dahlia had gotten him through it all, and now he was avoiding going home to her. He'd told her two weeks and he'd lost count of what month it even was now. All he knew was he'd probably lost her.

For the best, he kept telling himself. The woman deserved all the good in the world, and that was having a man who was there for her. How many of her smiles had he missed? All those nights he could have been holding her. Hell, he didn't know nearly enough about her, only that he'd never felt this way before. None of the Maddies, Kylas and Isabellas had kept him full of hope in that prison.

Sweet Dahlia... he had to go back to her. But not yet. First, he needed to shake what they'd done to him.

Water glistened on the dancing waves. The Gulf had always brought him solace, but today it was just water and the sand clinging to the hems of his jeans just grains. Neither was enough.

He shifted his jaw. It wasn't broken as he'd once thought, and the bruising had gone down considerably. His skin was fading from black and blue to green and yellow. A few more days of sunshine and he'd be ready.

After he'd been debriefed, they'd given him a cell phone but he'd yet to use it. How easy it would be to dial Dahlia. Hell, even if she was at work, he could call 911 again. A small smile twisted his lips. She'd been so pissed that he'd called there. He couldn't blame her, but her annoyance had only fired his blood.

For the first time since he'd last been with her, his cock stirred. If she walked up beside him right now, his chest would lose some of that empty hollowness and he'd pull her down on his lap, slanting his lips across hers as he stroked her body into a frenzy of need.

One call and he could make that connection again.

Leaning back in the sand, he fished the device out of his jeans. He'd kept it on silent so had missed the texts from his family.

Maman: When you're ready to come home, I'll have your favorite grits ready.

Tyler: *Hey, butthead. When you coming home to teach me how to ride that old motorcycle?*

He might have chuckled if he had it in him, but after the past weeks, laughter felt like foreign territory. And the last thing he was doing was teaching his little sister how to ride that bike. Ben continued thumbing through the messages.

Rocko: *I didn't get a chance to thank you before they dragged me out of there and onto a plane for surgery, but I will thank you now. If you hadn't slammed into that guy at the last minute, the bullet would have taken a much different path and I wouldn't be lying here convalescing with sexy nurse Addison bringing me drinks and giving me back rubs. Cheers, Cap'n. It's a pleasure serving with you.*

Sean: *When you get back, whattaya say about you, me, a couple of fishing poles and some bait? The catfish are biting.*

Ben swallowed hard and pushed himself to read them all. Each text a sort of get-well card, and they touched him.

Roades had sent a photo of his leg and a pretty woman posing over it, her skirt riding high on her tanned thighs.

Ben grunted with amusement. Typical Roades. Injured and living it up. The kid probably had a beer in one hand too.

Dylan: *I hope this eases your mind a bit – Chaz, Sean and I paid a visit to Lexi's asshole "friend." You don't need to worry about him anymore. He isn't even in the state.*

Sitting up straighter, Ben re-read that message. He didn't know what *he isn't even in the state* meant, but he wouldn't put anything past his brothers when it came to their little sis. She had wrapped them all around her fingers from birth, and each brother was more protective of her than the next, resulting in her own personal hitman squad. The fact that some men would prey on her weaknesses meant Ben would have to step it up. He needed to get more involved, watch over her more. Screen her boyfriends.

Not that their daddy didn't do a good job of that, greeting them at the door with a shotgun resting on his knees.

Chaz: *Dude, you are missing out on Maman's home-cooking. She's outdoing herself. Come home quick and we'll do some fishin'.*

Typical Chaz. Keeping things light when it was clear he was concerned about him. Ben pressed his lips together and read on.

Another from Dylan: *Catfish are hot right now. Come home and we'll go to the cabin. You can bring your girl.*

Ben's heart shot into his throat.

Sean: *I know Dylan let you in on the Lexi thing, but don't worry about anything. We took care of the guy.*

Damn, that didn't ease Ben's mind one damn bit. What the hell had his brothers done to the guy—trussed him up and tossed him in the swamp?

Sean again: *Lexi's pretty pissed. If she asks you, you don't know anything.*

"Jesus Christ," he muttered.

Maman: Your pére got the spit out and a hog ready to roast when you get home. We miss you, Ben.

Pére: Could use some help from someone who isn't full of estrogen to control these brothers of yours. Do you know what they did?

No, and Ben wasn't sure he wanted to. Maybe he'd never go home. The sun, sand and surf were all he needed.

Except it wasn't. He wanted to sit down at the dinner table to his *maman*'s good food and hear exactly what had gone down between his brothers and Lexi's boyfriend.

Lexi: *You guys all think you have to protect me, but when are you gonna learn that I can handle myself?*

Finally, a chuckle escaped Ben. If Lexi was giving sass, then she was okay.

Lexi: *Some woman called the house for you a few weeks ago. She didn't leave a message.*

He stopped breathing, just staring at the screen. Those little black letters held so much hope for him. Could it be Dahlia who'd called? He hadn't given her any number to contact him, but he knew her—she'd be resourceful.

With all the messages read, that chasm opened inside him once more. He was sitting here waiting for the things he loved to help him move on, when what he really needed was one woman who had made him forget before.

He stood, not bothering to dust the sand from his jeans. Then he raised a hand in salute to the water. He was going home and find Dahlia to let the healing begin.

Chapter Six

Dahlia ended her call with a happy sigh and leaned back in her seat to process what she'd just gone through. A life saved. A child crying happy tears. The world was good, at least for the moment.

A movement caught her eye, and she turned in time to see Joanie doing a weird walk-jog across the room to Dahlia's desk.

"What the...?"

Joanie grabbed her by the shoulders and leaned close to whisper, "There's someone outside who wants to see you."

She blinked. "Is it one of my friends? I can't leave my desk right now, but I could slip away and text her."

"No, no! It's not a girlfriend." Joanie waggled her brows.

Dahlia looked more closely at the older woman. She wore a flush over her face and appeared to be sweating a little. That could only mean...

She pushed back from her desk and shot to her feet. Joanie straightened too and they stared at each other.

"A big man? Green eyes?"

Joanie fluttered a hand in front of her face to fan away her perspiration. "My God, yes. Girl, if you don't go outside right now and talk to him, I'll personally pick you up and carry you out."

She threw a desperate look at her desk and touched her headset.

Joanie glanced around. "Kyle's on break. Just go. I'll cover you."

Impulsively, she leaned in and gave the woman a kiss on the cheek. "We find friends in unexpected places, don't we, Joanie?" Then she removed her headset and rushed away before her boss could spot her. If she was quick...

Heart thumping, she made it to the exit before realizing what she was doing.

She stopped dead, her palm on the cold metal door. Air conditioning hummed from the vents and outside the street would be a buzz of afternoon traffic. And Ben was there waiting for her.

Suddenly, she felt as if someone had dumped a shot of excitement into a martini shaker, along with a splash of arousal and followed it with a whole lot of irritation. After all this time he was here? Coming to do what? Lure her in with his smoky voice and a flash of his eyes? Would he grab her and kiss her up against the wall of the place where she worked, making it impossible for her to focus on her job for the rest of the day?

She had to face him or she wouldn't be able to concentrate. And the clock was ticking before Kyle returned from break.

She pushed open the door and looked around.

There, leaning against the building, arms folded across his chest and causing his biceps to bulge the sleeves of his T-shirt, was Ben Knight.

A breathy sigh left her, and she could have kicked her own ass if she could have gotten her foot that high. All those emotions started swirling around the cocktail shaker, until they were blended and she couldn't separate the flavors.

"You can't be here," she said, voice low and urgent.

He pushed away from the wall, his expression changing to one of total happiness.

Oh God, her heart felt that. The muscle fluttered uncontrollably.

"It's so good to set eyes on you," he rumbled, reaching for her.

She stepped back. "I'm working. I sneaked away but I only have a few seconds."

He moved his arm, and she caught sight of the bandage on his forearm. Her gaze flashed to his face, finally seeing the yellow of fading bruises and a red stripe across his throat she didn't even want to contemplate. Her stomach dropped.

"My God, what happened to you?"

He sliced his hand through the air as if what he'd done to get these injuries was nothing. But it wasn't nothing—he'd laid his life on the line to serve his country and in the meantime, she'd been a bitch about him not returning when she'd expected.

"Dahlia, honey, I've been thinking about you so much. I know you need to get back to work, but I couldn't wait until your shift was over to see you. Will you..." he caught her elbows and pulled her against his hard body until her nipples strained to get closer. "Will you let me kiss you once before you go back inside? Then I'll come back when you're finished working and we'll go somewhere. Eat something good. Look at the water or go catfishin'."

A perplexed smile tipped her lips. "Catfishin'?"

"Yeah. I don't care what we do—I just want to be with you. Please." The final word grated against her senses, and all she wanted was to go on tiptoe and kiss the hell out of this man.

She glanced at the deep cut above his brow and to one on his forehead, covered by the dark hair flopping over it. "Just tell me you're all right."

"I am now." He claimed her lips. The touch so tender that she feared his lips were bruised as well, but then he yanked her against him and crushed his mouth to hers. The searing heat of his body reached through her summery wrap dress, stroked her skin and reached deep into her chest and grabbed her heart.

133

He moved his lips back and forth over hers, not deepening the kiss with his tongue but content to explore her. This was a new side of Ben, and one she had to know more about.

Call her stupid, but what did she have to lose really? She could get her heart broken, but so what?

Trembling at his touch, she pulled away from the kiss. With her hands pressed to his hard chest, she said, "I have to go."

"I'll pick you up right here after work. What time do you get off?"

"I have a twelve-hour shift and I'm off at six."

"Then I'll be waiting." He caressed the hair off her cheek, studying her far too closely for a man who just wanted to bang.

On shaky legs, she went back inside and hurried to her desk. Kyle was nowhere in sight, but Joanie dropped her knitting and ran to her desk, surprisingly light on her feet for a woman who was nearing sixty.

"Tell me that man has a single daddy."

She opened her mouth to reply, and a laugh projected from it. She clapped her hand over her lips and shook her head. "I don't know anything about his parents, but he does have several brothers."

"Well, I can be a cougar if pressed to it." Joanie smoothed her hands over her full hips and Dahlia laughed again, feeling lighter than she had in a month. Just knowing Ben was okay seemed to be the injection of happiness she'd been missing.

"He's picking me up after my shift."

"Your lipstick's smeared," Joanie noted.

She brought her fingers back to her mouth, feeling the aftershocks of his kiss. Then she grabbed a tissue and wiped her lipstick off. She'd reapply it before he picked her up tonight.

Need rolled through her—she was almost giddy with it. For now, Ben was back and she could ride the high. Knowing how military men were, she'd soon come crashing down. Loving a man who served his country was like riding a gator—bumpy as hell. She had no idea if she was cut out for the lifestyle, but for now, she wasn't going to think about it.

She gripped the edge of her desk. "I just have to get through a few more hours of my shift."

Joanie nodded and shot her a smile as Kyle entered the room. He looked between the women as if trying to catch them at something, but he couldn't find anything to complain about in their flushed faces, so he returned to work.

Dahlia slid her headset back on and sat there for a long minute, daydreaming about seeing Ben after work. Falling into bed with him was so easy, but this time she'd actually like to spend time doing the things he suggested—going out to eat or even catfishing. But fishing would mean returning to her place to change clothes, and the bed would be ohhh, so close.

She covered her private smile with her hand, aware that her boss was staring at her again. Quickly, she picked up her knitting and took all her bottled energy out on the stitches.

The hours seemed to crawl by, and it didn't help that there weren't many calls to keep her busy. Of course, that was a good thing, but by the time Kyle told her to go home, she was on edge with anticipation.

After a quick trip to the restroom to fluff her hair, spritz herself with perfume and reapply lipstick that would stay put through dinner and as many kisses as Ben could dish out, Dahlia fought to keep herself from running out the door.

With her knitting bag and her purse slung over her shoulder, she exited the building. Her gaze shot to the place where Ben had been standing before, and a tingle spread through her lower belly.

Mother of God.

He'd cleaned up since she'd seen him. His jeans molded to his hard body, and his button-down shirt looked tailored for him. The blue stripes somehow clashed with his eyes and went all at the same time, and the cuffs were rolled over his veined forearms and the bandage he still wore.

He caught her looking and lifted his arm. "It's fine. I can remove the bandage, but it's itchy as hell while it heals. The bandage keeps me from digging at it, sort of like a dog wearing a cone."

Their gazes locked. In that heartbeat, a dozen emotions ran through her, but the most important was her need to sit next to him, hold his hand and hear whatever he had to say to her.

He took her hand and squeezed her fingers. "I've got my car this time."

"You mean I don't have to keep my skirt from flying up while I ride on the back of your bike?"

He slanted a look down at her. "That *was* hot as hell."

As they strolled away from the building, their bodies brushed together. She tried to walk in a straight line, but no matter what she did, her body seemed to have other ideas.

"I keep bumping into you." She laughed. The need to strip down in the middle of the street and let him take her was too strong to ignore. But if something besides sex was going to happen between them, they needed to do more than get naked.

"You'd better stop looking at me that way before I find an alley to take you in." His low voice shot sparks over her like fireworks scattering across a hillside.

She glanced away before she egged him on to do just that. "Maybe we'd better get some dinner quick then."

"Mm. I have a place that's out of the way in mind. It's a bit of a drive, but we can talk on the way."

She nodded. "Sounds great."

When he led her to an old pickup, she could only imagine how well he could reach between her thighs without a console of a newer model between them.

He paused, looking down at her. "I know what you're thinking."

Heat crept up her throat. "How do you know?"

"Because you chew your lip when you're turned on, and damn, I want to forego dinner and take you to bed. But I'm going to prove I can be a gentleman and hold a conversation that doesn't include a groan at the finish."

Her laugh was too throaty to say she was anything but ready for that primal noise. He opened the door and she slid into the truck. His scent filled the cab and there was a battered cowboy hat on the seat.

He got behind the wheel and shot her a grin that had her clenching her thighs.

"Is that your hat?"

"Yeah. Surprised?"

He plucked it off the seat and settled it on his head, eyes smoldering. "What do you think?"

"It suits you," she said honestly.

"I got used to it after spending summers at my uncle's place in Texas."

Leaving the hat on, he squeezed her thigh. How easy it would be to pick up where they'd left off that night in the SUV. Hell, she had her phone ready to video another sexy fingering session. But he seemed determined to stick to his word of being a gentleman. He pulled his hand off her leg and put it on the gearshift.

"Ready, honey?"

She nodded, heart too full to speak.

They zoomed off through the city and soon were headed into the bayou. When he pulled off at a roadside barbecue, she found herself surprised once more. What she knew of Ben was that he was a sweet-talkin' playboy who knew his way around her curves, so she'd expected some classy restaurant with expensive wine involved and not some barbecue in the bayou. Though, she had a feeling she was seeing the real Ben tonight.

"I sense you're surprised again," he said, cutting the engine.

"I realize that I don't know a lot about you, Ben."

He gave her a crooked grin. "That's what we're here for. C'mon." He got out and came around to her door before she could open it herself. Then he took her by the hand and parked her on a picnic table while he went to the window to order from the backwoods version of a food truck.

She sat admiring his jeans straining across his backside and the way his shirt hugged his shoulders as he extracted his wallet and paid for their meal. Then he took a seat across from her and reached for her hand. She stared at their entwined fingers lying on the rough wood.

"This place is great. I've never been here."

"Anatole has been feeding the Knights barbecue ever since I can remember." He nodded toward the window where the Creole could be seen giving orders to his workers in the roadside shack.

A waitress came out bearing drinks and then she took a minute to light a candle inside a Mason jar in the middle of the table.

"Haven't seen you in a while, Ben," the waitress drawled.

"Yeah, time passes quickly."

The waitress shot Dahlia a look. "Looks like you're all set, but if your brothers need some barbecue…" She smiled in a secretive way, "Tell them to come find me."

Ben nodded. "I'll do that." When the woman left, he grunted. "Sorry about that."

"I have a feeling she knows you pretty well." Dahlia arched a brow. Not even meeting one of Ben's ex-conquests could dampen her mood right now.

He shook his head. "Never had her in my bed, if that's what you're asking."

He reached for her fingers, entwining them. Dahlia stared into Ben's eyes. A long moment passed. For a long time, she'd been thinking about what she'd

140

say to him after he returned from his mission. And only two words ever came to mind.

Finally, she said, "Tell me."

* * * * *

Ben looked down at their hands and tried to think of what to say. He'd never stayed with one woman long enough to explain his job or even his life. But being here with Dahlia felt so right that he knew there was no other way than to let her in.

"Things didn't go great," he said.

"I figured." She inclined her head toward his bandaged arm.

"I can't tell you much, if anything at all. You know how it is, Dahlia."

"Yes, I do. I don't like it any more than my momma did, I'm guessing. She paced and worried every time my dad went away, but then he'd come home, and I'd see the love between them... Well, she knew nothing of what he did and they still had a life."

His heart jerked hard against his ribs. It took him a long second to recover from the shock of her words. "Are you saying you're willing to give us a try?"

She dropped her gaze. "I'm not sure, but..."

"You are," he said with confidence.

Her gaze snapped up. "Aren't you cocky?"

"Yes." He wasn't apologizing for it either.

Their food arrived and conversation turned to other topics, such as the loudness of the peeper frogs in the ditches along the road. Ben asked her about her job, and she clammed up.

"I'm sensing some stress with your work. Is it your boss? The one you were worried would find out you were outside with me?"

She shook her head. "Kyle's strict but could be worse. After all, we have a very serious job and a lot of people depending on us."

"Ah, so that's it."

She searched his face, a rib dripping with barbecue halfway to her mouth. "What's it?"

"You carry a lot home with you from your job."

"Maybe." She wiped the grease off her lips with a paper napkin. Then she said, "Don't you?"

More than she'd ever know. But being here with her, the night air wrapped around them and only a small candle in a Mason jar providing light in the falling darkness, he was rapidly putting that stress behind him.

"Silly question," she said. "I know you do."

"I saw your bag in the truck. Were those knitting needles I spotted?" His voice lilted into a tease that roused a smile from her. If anything, he hoped to wipe away her anxiety of a stressful job the same way she helped him. Just being together could be enough for both of them. At least he hoped.

She chuckled. "You got me. I'm old before my time."

He laughed. "I don't think that's true."

"It's a thing we all do at work. Between calls, we knit—even my weird boss."

"Hmm. Never heard of a guy knitting before."

She looked him over as if imagining him at work with a set of needles. "It's mindless, calming. It's easy to drop as soon as a call comes in and easy to pick up where you left off when you're finished with the call."

"So, did you save anybody today?" he asked, digging into his greens fried in bacon grease with a fork.

"Yes. Did you save anybody while you were away?"

He stared at her. "Just did my job is all."

She grew quiet. For a second, he worried his refusal to answer her questions would turn her away from him. But she took a bite and thoughtfully chewed.

"I'm sure you did, Ben, and it's okay if you don't want to tell me. But I do want to know why you asked me to wait and not to see Winters while you were gone."

He stiffened. "Did you see that jerk?"

She raised a brow. "Now he's a jerk? Hmm. Could it be you want me to be exclusive, Ben Knight?"

She was so adorable with a smear of barbecue on her lower lip and stray hairs twitching around her beautiful face in the Gulf breeze.

"Yes, he's a jerk. He's nothing but a POG, guarding an inactive base, and my guess is you could push him around, too."

"Why would I want to?"

"Exactly. You need someone who could handle shit when it goes south."

"Someone like you?" she asked.

He gave a nod. "Damn right. My shoulders are big enough to bear the weight of anything."

She skimmed her stare over his shoulders and across his chest, her lip caught in her teeth again. He released a growl and leaned across the table, more than ready to be finished with their meal.

"I asked you to wait so we could do more of *this*, Dahlia. And because I want you. I'm not going to pretend I don't want more with you."

"More?"

"More of this." He waved between them, causing the flame to leap in the glass at the increase of oxygen. "More of your sweet lips... and my tongue buried in your pussy."

Her mouth fell open on a puff of air. "Ben."

"Are you finished eating? Because I'm so hungry for dessert that I can't sit here another second."

He got her off the picnic bench and halfway to the truck before he couldn't hold back anymore. He swept her off her feet but didn't hesitate before he was kissing her.

* * * * *

Ben climbed behind the wheel and looked at her through the darkness. Dahlia felt like her body was humming, the first soft whisper of more. She gripped the seat, shivering under his gaze. He didn't move to touch her or continue that burning kiss he'd just laid on her.

He ran a hand through his hair. "My family has a cabin. We could be alone there." His gritty tone heightened her need.

She nodded. "Is it far?"

He cocked a brow. "Eager to jump my bones?" Not waiting for an answer, he put the truck into gear and took off onto the highway. The crepe myrtles were draped with Spanish moss and the occasional marsh hawk swept out of the darkness after its prey.

Suddenly, Dahlia felt as if she was sitting beside a stranger. Whether it was the sexual tension fogging the air or a true panic at what he'd said to her back at the roadside restaurant was anybody's guess.

He wanted more? What did that mean? One part of her was saying he was all wrong for her—that she wasn't entering a relationship with a man who might not come home to her one day. But her mind was telling her to just look at the man sitting there with his thick shoulders and broad chest, his long fingers on the wheel inciting need in her she couldn't control.

So, would she stomp on her heart for a chance at that sexy body?

Hell yes, she would. And everything that came with it.

He was a jungle gym and she wanted to climb all over him and lick every inch too. The way his hair tumbled into his eye and even the bob of his Adam's apple was damn masculine. Maybe they didn't need to reach the cabin, after all. She could just scoot across the seat and duck her head while unzipping his fly…

Did she want to be another woman who gave a hot guy road head? Well, who cared if she was? Damn, now she was wetter *and* overthinking.

He kept his hands on the wheel and his eyes off her, directed at the road illuminated by the headlights. His demeanor didn't give any hint that he was actually happy about taking her to this family cabin of his.

She fidgeted on the seat, and he threw her a look—eyes hooded in a dark and utterly panty-soaking way.

"So you *do* want me," she said.

He did a double-take. "What would give you the idea I don't? I'm practically dying over here for you." He took her wrist and smashed her hand over the front of his jeans and the massive erection there.

She sucked in a breath.

"I'm trying to be a gentleman and not fuck you along the road, Dahlia. I want to show you something more, but you're killing me just with the way you're looking at me. And fuck, I can smell your arousal."

A tingle of heat spread into a wave. She clenched her thighs together. Under her hand, still pressed to his cock, his erection seemed to throb. She curled her fingers around it and he tugged her hand away, keeping hold of it on the seat between them.

He threw her another glance. "Do you have any damn idea how much of a temptation you are sitting there in that sexy wrap dress with your cleavage begging for my tongue all night? Or the way you widen your eyes a little and lick your lips while I'm talking? It's distracting as hell and all I want to do is bend you over and fuck you."

Practically panting, she managed to say, "Doesn't sound so bad to me."

He let go of her hand to run his over his face, as if wiping away any lust she'd see there. He may be good at masking his expressions, but she knew Ben's lustful stares like she knew the freckles smattering her own collarbones.

When he cast her another look, he let out a rough groan. "Dammit, woman. I'm trying to take this slow and make it right for once. Help me out."

His plea caught her off guard and she tossed her head back with a laugh. "All right, I won't tell you that I considered laying my head in your lap and unzip—"

He swerved on the empty road for no good reason, but she wasn't sorry for the chance to tease him.

Leaning closer to the windshield, she peered into the night. "Did a bobcat just step out? I'm glad you didn't hit it."

A throatier growl left him but he didn't speak. She liked the thought that she'd stripped all the words from him and as soon as he stopped driving, he'd have all those slick moves of his body for her. Right now, she couldn't wait for the scorching-hot brainless fucking only he could give her.

He managed to drive for another thirty minutes before taking a right turn onto a dirt road. Thick mud sucked at the truck tires and even the moon didn't seem to penetrate this part of the bayou. The headlights panned over the side of the road and she swore she saw the red glinting eyes of a gator.

"This is off the beaten path," she commented.

"That's the point." His words came out soft.

Need rolled through her, and she managed to keep from diving for his fly. How the tables turned and she was now respecting a hot guy's request to go slow, she had no idea. This must be fate's sick joke on her.

"Your family owns this?"

He nodded but didn't say more until the headlights struck a small cabin clinging to the edge of the waterway. A good rain looked as if it would flood it, if not for the stilts it was built on.

He stopped the truck, and she looked at the swamp between the truck and the cabin.

"How do we get there?" she asked.

He was staring at her, and her heart tripled in speed under his direct stare. "I pull us there in a pirogue."

A thrill ran through her. She might be a Louisiana girl, but she'd never done this herself. Though she'd heard of people who lived deep in the swamps traveling by pirogue, and she was enchanted.

He reached for her hand, and she placed it in his big, warm one. "Ready?"

Her nipples peaked against her bra. She couldn't think of anything she'd rather do than spend a night at this isolated cabin with the hottest special ops guy on the planet. "Yes."

He got out and she did too. When he circled the truck to take her hand, he said, "Watch your footing. This place isn't exactly right for those shoes."

"I wasn't thinking of bayous when I got dressed this morning."

"It's okay." He eyed her platform heels. "They're sexy as hell and I can't wait to take them off you and kiss you from your ankles up. Now stop here." He left her standing on a bank and she hoped like hell that red-eyed creature she'd spotted along the road hadn't slithered this direction.

Ben was only a dark figure as he rustled through some weeds and came out with a long pole. "Good. My brothers didn't drop the pole into the water like they sometimes do when in a hurry to leave." He did something that made a scraping noise and then walked back to her.

When he was within her orbit, she felt his pull on her. Then he stopped in front of her and leaned in, lips by her ear. "I'm going to carry you so you don't get your feet wet." Without waiting for her agreement, he picked her up and she forgot all about the romantic beauty of their surroundings and savored the feel of being in his strong arms, against his big chest and enveloped by his clean smell.

His boots scuffed as he stepped onto the flat-bottomed boat with the shallow sides that would be their transportation to the rustic cabin. He set her on her feet and she gripped him to gain her balance.

"Oh fuck." He crouched and made a quick move she couldn't exactly make out in the darkness. But when he stood and she spotted the long curled shape of a snake in his hands, she released a bottled scream.

He flung the snake into the water and it made a splash. Small ripples caught the faint moonlight streaming through a break in the swamp trees.

"It's okay now. Sorry about that. I should have checked before I set you down."

She wrapped her arms around her middle and rubbed the chill off her upper arms.

"You all right?" She couldn't see his face but heard the smile in his voice.

"Yes," she breathed out.

"Good. If you haven't ridden in a pirogue before, you can sit or stand."

She glanced at the blackness pooling around her feet. How he could see better in the darkness than her was probably due to his training. Who knew what the man did in the dark.

Well, she did know a bit…

"I'll stand."

"Okay. Then why don't you get behind me and put your arms around me. That's it. Now brace your legs apart a bit so you have more balance."

She mirrored his stance, though his leg spread was much wider. With her arms tight around his waist, she felt anchored.

"Ready?" He had the pole in hand and when he felt her nod, he dug the pole into the swamp bottom, propelling the pirogue along.

With each move of the pole, his back muscles rippled. She leaned her cheek against his spine and breathed in, staring at the mysterious swamp they drifted through. The cabin was only a short distance, and the pirogue bumped something wooden. A dock.

"I can't wait to see this in the daylight."

"It's a swamp," he said, obviously unattached to the beauty. He dropped the pole onto the dock and twisted to pull her into his arms, plucking her off her feet and setting her onto firmer footing.

"This is an interesting way to reach a destination."

He bent to tie off the pirogue with a rope around a metal hook. "At least you know I won't be running out on you before morning."

She wrapped her arms around herself again, this time to hold in the warmth oozing through her. Part of her was scared to do that—wake up with Ben. It would push them toward that intimacy he claimed he wanted and she still hadn't yet processed.

When he stood, he grabbed her by the hand and led her blindly across the short dock to a ramp that meandered to the cabin. They paused before a door, and in the darkness she couldn't see how he opened it. For all she knew, he'd used Cajun black magic. She wouldn't put any skills past this man.

He fiddled with something and then pushed open the door. It gave a pleasant creak of welcome, making her think of summer nights and porch swings. A second later, he turned on a battery-powered light.

A warm yellow halo wreathed them, and she blinked at the brightness. "I'm not accustomed to seeing things in the dark."

He only smiled and drew her inside. That odd feeling between them was back—like they were strangers meeting for the first time. It excited her. Was this how her momma had felt each time her daddy had returned from a mission?

Ben closed the door and moved close to her. He wasn't even a little out of breath after poling them through the swamp. He took her by the shoulders and leaned down until his lips were an inch from hers.

Falling into those green eyes of his was easy—too easy. But she'd come here willingly, and she'd take what she could from the experience. Tomorrow would be soon enough to figure out her course and nurse any bruising on her heart. Because surely, this man wasn't meant for her. It was sweet talk, pillow talk—and didn't he know he didn't need those things to get her into his bed?

Too many conflicting emotions whirled through her brain. For now, she needed to let all of her misgivings go and just be in the moment.

She slipped her arms around his neck and her breasts brushed against his very firm body.

"Dahlia, you're so beautiful." His gaze flicked over her face and hair as if drinking in her appearance, and her heart gave a small tug.

"And I've never seen a more gorgeous man in my life," she admitted, watching his lips because she wanted them the most. On her own lips, on her breasts, belly… and lower.

He stroked her long hair, twisting a lock in his fingers. "I won't run out on you tonight. Tonight, it's just the two of us and nothing can interfere."

Dammit, his sweet talk was getting the best of her. Warmth pooled around her heart.

Going on tiptoe, she waited for his kiss, but it didn't come. He seemed content to stare at her and just hold her. The longer they stood there, the more the feeling of being with a stranger heightened.

"I'm Dahlia," she said foolishly.

A small smile tipped the corner of his lips. "Nice to meet you. I'm Ben. Does this mean we're starting over?"

Controlling her urge to shiver at his words, she lifted a shoulder in a shrug. "If that's what you want."

He gave a light shake of his head. "I don't want to bury the moments we've had already, but I need you to know right now that I meant what I said about wanting more, honey. You make me feel..." He trailed off as if unsure of how to put it into words.

Gripping him tighter, she drew him down. "Just kiss me, Ben."

He nodded, nose brushing hers. When he leaned in millimeter by millimeter to settle his lips over hers, electricity and passion bloomed out from the place their lips were joined. She held him tighter and pressed her body closer.

The feel of him, the flavor, the scent... all mixed together, forming a blaze of sensation in her brain.

She wasn't going to even think that the emotions were colored pink and had little red hearts dotted all over them.

She dragged in a breath, dizzy and burning up for this man.

He planted a hand unapologetically on her ass, kneading her flesh through her flimsy dress and deepening the kiss. Hesitantly moving his lips across hers and then nibbling lightly. When she sank her teeth into his lower lip to urge him along, he chuckled, the sound so carefree that she tumbled a little deeper into the moment.

With a rough groan, he parted her lips with his tongue and plunged inside. Need spiked. She mewled and pasted herself to his body. Hands roving over his strong back and down to his chiseled waist and lower to his rock-hard ass. He inched up the hem of her dress, exposing her thighs and backside to the humid cabin air as he ravished her mouth.

When he eased a finger under the elastic of her thong, she cried out for more.

He broke the kiss and stared down at her, chest heaving. Her head swam.

"I'm going to love you all night long, honey."

"So much talk and so little action," she cooed, going on tiptoe again for another kiss.

He vibrated out a laugh and started walking backward with her, somehow navigating around furniture of a small living room and past a big rough-hewn table that looked large enough to seat a big family or a lot of guests.

"You've done this before," she said, not breaking their stare.

His brow crinkled. "What do you mean?" He sidestepped an end table holding an oil lamp.

"Brought women here before."

He shook his head. "Never. I always kept that part of my life separate." At least he wasn't insulting her by denying he'd *had* other women. Though the idea unsettled her.

When they reached a short hallway, he opened the first door and pulled her inside.

Moonlight spilled through one window, shimmering across a patterned quilt.

He gazed down at her. "God, Dahlia. I want you."

The gritty admission undid her, and she wasn't going slow for another second. She ripped off his shirt and went at his body like kissing each swell and dip of his chest and abdomen would bring about world peace.

Need blasted through her as she reached the yummy love trail leading down into the waist of his jeans. She set her tongue on the trail and dropped to her knees to stare up at him. "Take off your jeans. I want to suck your cock."

* * * * *

156

Fucking hell, he was going to explode. Dahlia's soft lips pouted and her eyes flashed up at him. From her position kneeling at his feet, he had a clear view down her dress and the swells of her breasts made him think of sinking his cock between them and feeling all that warmth and softness.

His mind reeled.

When he didn't obey her womanly command, she took matters into her own hands and unbuttoned his jeans. The zipper sliding down was the most erotic sound he'd ever heard.

Her warm breath came in pants across his briefs, and his eyes rolled back in his head. He sank his fingers into her thick hair and drew her head to him as she fingered down the waist of his briefs and his cock sprang free.

She nuzzled it and he damn near lost his mind. "Jesus," he breathed out.

Dahlia snaked out her tongue and lapped at the head of his cock. His slit pooled with juices, and he let out a groan.

"Keep that up and—" He broke off as she swallowed his cock head. Liquid heat shot to his balls and he yanked her in, sinking his shaft to the back of her throat.

She moaned around him, and his control slipped precariously. He clenched his hands in her hair, and she released another throaty noise.

He swayed his hips backward, pulling out of her mouth. But she grabbed his ass and jerked him back in, swallowing him to the root.

"Fuck. Holy hell." He stared down at her. Hollowed cheeks and wide eyes glistened up at him with lust. He was losing it. If he didn't pull out now, he was going to blow in her mouth and then he couldn't be responsible for holding her in place to swallow every drop of his cum.

She sucked him in again, tongue dancing up his length to flick over the tip and all without withdrawing on his cock. Jesus, at this rate he'd have a Cajun *pêtre* in here to marry them. Walking away from a woman who could use her tongue in ways like this was not an option.

When she cupped his balls and stroked the sensitive flesh, he jerked away. She yanked him back and sucked him in again.

"Oh God, honey. I can't. Stand up here." Using his hands in her hair, he brought her to her feet. He cradled her face and swooped in to kiss her. The flavors of himself on her mouth only drove him crazier.

He stripped off her dress and left her in only bra, panties and high heels. He rocked back to look at her. Moonlight kissed her curves in all the right places, imprinting them on his mind. His cock throbbed against his abs, and she dropped her gaze to it, licking her lips once more.

"Hellll, don't do that, honey. I'm barely holding onto my control." In seconds, he tore away her bra and palmed her full breasts while searching her eyes. "These perfect tits need my tongue."

"Mmm." A shudder ran through her, and he bent to the task. With short licks over her breast to the center peak and sucking it into his mouth with soft pulls until she gasped and clutched at his head. Then he moved to the other breast and showered kisses over it.

"Suck it, please, Ben."

He did better than that—he grazed the tip with his teeth and she cried out, shaking in his hold.

He couldn't wait another second. He tossed her onto the bed, cradling her head in one hand and lowering her to the pillow. They shared a wild tangling of tongues before he moved down her body, kissing each inch of flesh he came in contact with. As he reached that tiny thong, his mouth watered to think of what was beneath.

Her breaths hitched, and he knew she was as crazy for him as he was her. Balls about to burst, he eased down her thong, hooked her legs over his shoulders and sank his tongue into her sweet, wet pussy.

* * * * *

In her experience, most men didn't want to perform oral, but Ben had done it every. Single. Steaming-hot. Time.

He trailed his tongue up and down her slit like it was his life's work, and she couldn't hold still if she tried. Her hips rose off the bed without her mind telling them to, and she jerked against his mouth each time he reached her clit. Need climbed and she stopped thinking and only felt.

He clutched her hips and wagged his tongue back and forth. A cry struck her as she rocketed sky-high but he backed off, keeping her away from what she needed most.

She thumped a balled fist on the bed. "Ben!"

Was he chuckling? The asshole.

Locking a hand to his nape, she yanked him down where she wanted him. He changed his rhythm, lapping slowly, tenderly. Each strum of his tongue against her folds made that knot in her belly pull tight. When he opened his mouth over her clit and sucked it with extreme gentleness, she quivered.

Maybe this was better than demanding he take her fast and hard.

He watched her up the length of her body, and she couldn't tear her gaze from his tongue moving over her clit, back and forth. Up and down. Back and —

Her pussy contracted hard and her orgasm hit out of nowhere. She bowed upward, and he drew on her clit as the bundle of nerves short-circuited and ecstasy swept over her.

Dizzy from not breathing, she gasped on a final cry but her hips continued to twitch upward to the soft caresses of his tongue.

"You're… so fucking… good at that," she panted.

"Mmm. We're well-matched then, because your mouth was sending me straight to hell."

"Next time I'm finishing you," she declared, staring at him boldly.

He laughed as he donned a condom and poised over her, lips glistening with her juices. "I'll take you up on that offer. But right now, I want this pussy."

He moved her leg upward, resting her calf on his muscled shoulder, and slid inside in one slick move.

The angle— Oh God, how did he know he was hitting that spot? She was already shaking and on the verge of coming.

His eyes hooded as he did an erotic pushup, withdrawing to the tip and gliding back in over that sweet spot. Again and again. She wanted to gallop off to the finale her body craved, but he'd taught her a lesson just now with his mouth—good things came to those who waited.

She sank her teeth into her lip and watched his handsome face contort with the bliss he was experiencing. Knowing he liked how her pussy hugged his cock only sent her racing to the end again.

When she came apart, he took his time, watching her tremble and finally leaned in to kiss her with all the passion she needed at that final moment.

Panting, she lay there like a dead person. But Ben wasn't finished with her.

He turned her over onto her stomach and stuffed a pillow under her belly. The position smacked her with awareness. That time he'd fingered her ass and it had felt so good, but... was she ready for more if he asked for it?

She could almost feel his gaze washing over her behind. Then he touched her cheeks, running his hands up and down them. When he pulled them apart and cool air struck her most intimate spot, she sucked in sharply.

"Shh. I've got you. I promise not to do anything you don't want. When I take this ass, you'll be warmed up for me, believe me."

Oh, she had no doubt that she'd be begging him like some wanton slut. And that he'd do things to her body that she'd never imagined.

She shivered and clutched at the sheets as he ran a fingertip over her pucker.

"Fuck, what I wouldn't give for some lube." His words sounded with the roughness of need, and suddenly, she wanted to offer herself up to him completely.

But he was right—they needed to prepare for such an event.

He swirled his fingertip around and around her pucker, and her pussy flooded. Then he moved, and a second later something warm and infinitely wet was at her backside.

He was tonguing her.

"Oh my… Gawwwwd." She shook.

He delivered short strokes of his tongue around and around, taking the same path his finger had. When he sank into her slightly, she squeezed her eyes shut, clinging to the edge of insanity.

"Ben!"

"I want to make you come with my tongue but I'm going to fucking blow my load if I don't get inside you." He shifted again, and all at once his cock head bulged against her pussy folds.

With one arm wrapped around her waist, he drove inside her and drew her up to meet his thrust.

* * * * *

Don't blow. Don't blow. Don't blow.

The mental chant was doing nothing for his control. Especially with the exciting and musky taste of her on his tongue and knowing she was so responsive to anal play with him. Not to mention knowing she was a virgin there and when he took her ass, it would be a claiming unlike any before.

His gut clenched as heat swept up from his balls. She was so tight, so hot. And now she was gripping

163

him tighter with her inner walls, her sweet pussy sucking at him almost.

He ground his teeth to hold back, but there was no use. She was tearing away his last shred of control.

With a roar, he threw his head back and poured jet after jet of cum into her pulsating pussy, aware that she was emitting those tormenting cries of release too, their coupling more complete than he could even dream.

His mind blanked as he spouted another hard shot and he hung over her, on the verge of collapse.

What the hell was this woman doing to him?

He lowered her to the bed gently and pressed a kiss to the side of her neck. She didn't move.

Then got up and went to the bathroom, taking care of the condom and swishing his mouth with mouthwash. When he returned, she lay in the same position.

"Did I kill you?" he asked.

Her shoulders moved with a laugh. "Yes. You can hide my body in the swamp."

"Wouldn't be the first time such a thing was discussed in this cabin."

She twisted to crack an eye up at him. He chuckled and lay down next to her, pulling her into his arms with her head resting on his shoulder.

"Maybe you'd better explain your last statement. I can't tell what a man like you is capable of, Ben."

He laughed again. How she made him feel so carefree after the shit he'd been through was nothing short of miraculous. "My brothers are a rough lot," he said in explanation.

"Hmm. Were those guys all your brothers? The ones at my father's barbecue?"

"All but one. Rocko is part of our team." He feared saying too much and turned the topic. Running his finger down her arm, he grew fascinated by the gooseflesh he raised in his wake. "About what I did a little bit ago."

She stilled. "What's that?"

"When I tongued your ass."

A shiver coursed through her, making her shift against him. His cock hadn't yet settled and bobbed against his abs once more.

"What about it?" Her tone was shy.

He cupped her chin and raised her gaze to meet his. "Did you like it?"

"I— I've never had that done before."

"I know."

"How can you know?"

"I can tell by your reactions to me."

"Cocky, aren't you?"

"Yes."

She pushed out a breath that was more like a hidden laugh. "Fine. Yes, I liked it. It makes me feel out of control and centered on you at the same time. Does that make sense?"

She could never know how her words struck him. So perfect, so true. They explained exactly how he felt each time he was with her. Damn, he'd known back at the roadside restaurant over that flickering candle on the picnic table that he was falling for her. It was what spurred him to tell her he wanted more, and the fact he wasn't back-peddling to take those words back meant that he was really in deep shit.

Ben Knight didn't do relationships. He did women—lots of them.

Except when he was with this particular woman. Then he never wanted to leave her bed.

How to hold onto her was another problem altogether. He could snipe a man before he killed one of his team members, could blow shit up without remorse, but he could not bear to hurt Dahlia.

In his line of work, he had no idea if he could keep from doing that. Hell, even this last mission had gone so sideways it was almost horizontal. What if he made promises to her and then never came back? He couldn't leave a widow behind.

Then how long before some asshole like Winters moved in to take his place? He nearly growled. He couldn't begin to think of some other man claiming her while he wasn't even on earth to stop it.

Fuck, he was really far gone.

And she was asleep. His little dark-haired angel was cuddled against his chest, long lashes casting shadows across her cheeks and tearing his heart out with each soft breath she took.

Somehow, he had to figure out a way to cling to this. To hold onto her and continue to be the captain of Knight Ops. Half the night, he lay awake listening to the frogs peeping in the swamps and the water lapping at the cabin supports, but Ben could not figure out a way to keep Dahlia and not hurt her in the long run. Only one answer surfaced time and again, and it was selfish as hell.

He'd have to retire his position of captain and leave the force.

Chapter Seven

There was nothing sexier than a half-naked man standing barefoot on a dock pulling fish out of the water for her lunch.

Ben unhooked another fish and dropped it into a bucket sitting on the dock.

Dahlia wrapped her arms around her knees and smiled to herself. "You know, there's something so erotic about a man who can protect *and* provide."

He shot her a look over his shoulder. "That so?"

"Mmm-hmm."

"Well," he said, dropping the line into the water again, "there's something so erotic about a woman wearing nothing but your shirt while watching you provide."

Her smile widened. The shirt he spoke of hung to her knees and off one shoulder. She couldn't deny she felt sexy wearing it. And more than a few flutters of emotion too. After last night...

The swamp and cabin in the daylight was exactly what she'd pictured. Wild, primitive—a little like Ben himself, and from what she'd seen of his brothers at that party, she imagined the whole family to be the same.

She watched Ben unhook another fish.

"So what's for lunch besides fish?"

"Could rustle up some turtle eggs if you're up for it."

She didn't like the thought of little turtles not hatching because she'd eaten them for lunch.

"Or a gator," Ben continued. "There's one lazing on the rock over there."

She got up and stood beside him to follow his finger where he pointed to a rock beneath a branch sagging under the weight of Spanish moss.

The creature looked small enough for Ben to take down, but then again, she figured the man could take on much larger beasts and most likely had. But the tiny spikes of its skin and long tail swishing back and forth as it sunned itself didn't appeal to her taste buds.

"I think the fish will be enough."

He flashed a grin. "You sure? If you don't want to eat the gator, I could make you a purse or some shoes."

"Definitely not."

He reeled her in with an arm around her shoulders and anchored her to his side. They stood together in the sun, looking over a world she didn't see every day with a man she had no idea if she'd see again.

This idea kept jumping into her brain. How had her parents' marriage survived such conditions?

Standing next to the shirtless, barefoot man didn't seem the time to think on it, so she pushed the thoughts from her mind.

"Does your family come here often?"

"As often as we can. We're all busy, in separate parts of the country even. Though now we have more opportunities."

She nodded. Her cheek against his warm arm.

"My parents and sisters come here more often."

"Sisters?" she asked in surprise. "You didn't mention sisters."

"Twins." He flipped another fish out of the water. They were small and a man of his size probably needed a lot to fill him up.

She recalled the woman who'd answered the phone that time she'd called the Knights', and she'd asked to take Dahlia's message. Had that been one of the sisters? Now Dahlia felt like a bitch for thinking the worst of Ben, that he had other women on the sidelines.

She had to ask the thing that had been niggling at her all day. "Ben, how long can we really stay here? Won't they be trying to get ahold of you?"

He looked down into her eyes. "Meaning your father with another mission?"

She nodded, stomach hurting and the idea of freshly fried fish no longer appetizing.

"Believe it or not, there is cell service, even if there isn't electricity out here. They know how to reach me if they need to." His gaze sharpened. "But I didn't think to ask about you. Do you need to get back for work?"

"No, it's my day off. Tomorrow I have a twenty-four-hour shift."

He raised his brows. "That's a long shift."

She nodded. Those times were harder because she had no way to escape the stresses. And a lot could happen in twenty-four hours.

"Can I ask you something about your job, honey?"

"Of course," she said. "Even though I'm not allowed to ask about yours."

He gave a hint of a smile and continued, "Do you enjoy what you do or is it just a job? Something to pay the rent?"

She brushed her hair off her face, considering his question. "It's difficult many times, but there are joys too."

"That's not what I'm asking. I want to know if the stress gets to you too much."

"What makes you think I'm stressed?"

"I saw your face yesterday, honey. When you came outside, there were lines on your forehead and I know seeing me didn't put them there. And after I picked you up, I could see you slowly cast off the worries after we'd been together for a while."

She swallowed. Was she that transparent?

"It's high stress, yes. But I love it. I do," she insisted, meeting his stare.

"All right. I believe you. I just don't want you stressed out. If there's something else you can do for an income, I'd encourage you to find that."

She didn't know how to take his suggestion. Was he being concerned or high-handed? She couldn't help but wonder if he was thinking of himself. On days she had long shifts, she couldn't see him even if he was in town. They had yet to encounter that problem, but Ben wasn't stupid. He would have thought of it.

And what about the times she was off work and wanted to spend time with him, but he was off disarming criminals and taking down terrorists or whatever else he did?

She couldn't dwell on the topic any longer. She looked into the bucket. "Do you think that's enough?"

"Depends on how big your appetite is, but yes, I think it will do." He removed his fishing line from the water and sat cross-legged on the dock to clean the fish, tossing the inedible parts back into the water for the gators. They surfaced one by one to feast, and Dahlia inched her toes back from the edge of the dock as they did.

"You asked how long we can be here, and I've been thinking, honey."

She looked to him. His green eyes seemed to glow in the sunlight and the green surroundings. "What's that?"

"We could leave after lunch. Go back to my family's home. Pay them a visit." He paused. "If you'd like, that is."

Oh God, he was asking her to meet his family? This was barreling too fast. She wasn't ready for anything more than having a fried fish lunch and maybe another roll in the hay with the muscled man.

"Tell you what," he said as if sensing her hesitation. "Let's eat. Then I'm going to take you back to bed and make you scream my name a half dozen more times." When he grinned, the sun dimmed because he was the only light she saw. "Then if you want to go back to my family's house for dinner, I'm sure my mother will love to meet you."

"Who's to say she'd have enough to feed us? She doesn't know we're coming."

He gave a light shake of his head. "You don't know my mother."

* * * * *

Ben lifted Dahlia's leg into the air, admiring the sexy curves of calf, the sloping rise of her knee, those strong inner thighs that could clamp around a man and make him forget... well, everything.

From the tangle of bedding she rested upon, she gazed up at him, a slight smile brushed over her beautiful lips. With her hair spread over the pillows, she could be a mermaid or a Cajun voodoo priestess. One look and a man was on his knees, begging to serve her.

Ben included.

He turned his lips against her calf and kissed his way to her ankle. Flicking his tongue over her dainty ankle bone.

"Do you have an obsession with ankles or just my ankles?" Her voice was throaty, he liked to think from the screaming orgasm he'd just given her.

"I'm pretty obsessed with this part too." He sank his teeth lightly into her calf and then her knee, working his way up to her inner thigh. A stuttering breath escaped her as he tongued a line straight to her soaking pussy.

She sucked in a gasp, but he heard something else. A light bump of wood on the dock.

He shot out of bed, had on his briefs and snatched up his gun before Dahlia could even track him with her eyes.

"What is it?" She bolted upright.

"Someone's here." In stealth mode, he moved to the window, weapon at the ready. He peeked around the frame but all he could make out was the trees and water. The only view of the dock was from the other side of the cabin.

"Stay put," he ordered Dahlia.

"What!" Her feet hit the floor and she snatched at the nearest thing she could throw on, which was his shirt. He barely registered the flurry of her movements as he sneaked to the door, his steps deadly silent.

There it was—another bump of wood on wood. He'd been sleeping in this cabin since he could walk, and he'd never heard of a log falling into the water and floating against it, but there was always a first.

There were also thieves, terrorists, gunmen and hitmen.

With one finger, he pushed the door open and stepped into the hall.

A girly squeal had his heart leaping into his throat and pounding so hard he felt it must be expanding his neck like a bullfrog. With a grating sigh, he lowered the weapon and safety'd it.

"Jesus, Lexi, what the hell are you doing here?"

Behind her, more people were pouring through the cabin door. The whole family, in fact.

She grinned and threw her arms around him. "I'm so glad to see you, Ben. We know how you can get stuck inside your head and that you'd come to the cabin. So we came to keep you compan—" She broke off, looking behind Ben.

He didn't need to turn to know Dahlia stood behind him—his family was all gawking at her like they'd thought he was gay all these years.

Turning, he extended an arm for her to come into. She must be nervous as hell. Meeting his family was daunting enough when you hadn't just been interrupted by them, thinking they were invaders and after having Ben's tongue in her pussy.

He could still taste her.

She moved forward with shoulders back and head high, wearing only his T-shirt like a queen wore bejeweled robes. No wonder he was so fascinated by her. She was freakin' perfect.

"Everyone, this is Dahlia."

His brothers grinned and exchanged looks. Chaz held out a hand, and the other guys slapped twenty-dollar bills into his palm. He thanked them and pocketed the cash.

"Great to see you again, Miss Jackson," Sean said.

Ben arched a brow at the amusement in Sean's tone. He'd get whatever was tickling his brother's fancy out of him soon enough.

Directing his attention to the Knights who hadn't yet met Dahlia, he said, "Maman, Pére, Tyler, Lexi... this is Dahlia."

Lexi's face split into a wide smile. "Are you the one who called the house looking for Ben the other week?"

Dahlia shifted. "Um, yes. Well, I'm going to get dressed." She threw a wave that was at last showing her nerves and practically dove back into the bedroom.

Ben pushed out a sigh. "Ya'll couldn't have warned me you were coming?"

"Get dressed, Ben. Nobody wants to see you in your skivvies," Tyler drawled, running her fingers through her long brown tresses.

"I'll be right back. Hope you know there's no food up here. We didn't bring any—been livin' off fish."

His father finally rubbed the smirk off his lips. "There's always something to eat in these swamps, and it's been an age since I've had me a fine, roasted gator. But lucky for you, we brought a few coolers of food with us and we'll share. I don't think that tiny slip of a woman's going to eat much."

Ben grunted. "I'm going to change."

As soon as he walked into the bedroom, he found Dahlia just sitting on the side of the bed, staring at her hands. She looked dazed and so beautiful the sight made his heart give a painful squeeze.

"*Cher*... what is it?" He sank to his knees before her and gripped her hands, searching her face for the despair he expected. What woman wanted to walk out of the bedroom to find her lover's huge family had joined them in their private getaway? Hell, he'd wanted to run for the hills after learning Colonel Jackson was her father.

She tipped her face up and smiled. Then laughed. Her giggles took hold and she threw herself back on the mattress, curving onto one side to hold in her laughter.

Relief swept him as he crawled onto the bed with her. Slipping his arms around her, he drew her into the pocket of his body where she fit so perfectly. "You're not upset then?"

"I guess if I didn't know what I was getting into when your brothers practically kidnapped me at my own father's birthday barbecue to force me to talk to you, I know now." Another choke of laughter left her, and she dug her knuckles into her teeth.

He rocked back to look at her. "I think you're hysterical, honey. Seeing my family does that to everyone."

She laughed harder, and he joined her for a long, breathless moment. Then a crash sounded and a raised voice followed—one of his brothers telling off another for dropping something.

Ben sobered. Staring at the pink-faced woman in his arms, he stroked her hair off her temple. "You sure you're okay with this? We can still escape."

"No." She shook her head. "Let's get dressed and meet them before they think I'm rude. It's bad enough they saw me wearing only your shirt and... Well, you know what I *wasn't* wearing."

He cocked a brow and grinned down at her. "Oh, I know, honey." He leaned in closer, but before he could kiss her, she planted her hands on his chest and pushed him back.

Watching her dress was a turn-on like nothing else, especially since he'd only seen her get out of clothes, never put them on. He loved the little shimmies she did to get her dress hem to fall into place around her knees and the care she took knotting the tie at her waist.

Finally, she raked her fingers through her hair and turned to him. "Do I look like someone you'd bring home to *Maman*?"

"Honey, I'd bring you home wrapped in a feed sack. You're gorgeous no matter what. But before we go out there and face the grilling we're sure to get, promise me something." He searched her eyes.

"Anything."

"That you won't walk away based on what's about to take place."

She blinked. "You think I'll dump you because of one meeting with your family?"

He considered if that was what he meant and then nodded. "They can get wild here at the cabin. You might see a side of us that you don't want to know. But that isn't me... not all the time, anyway." He dashed a hand through his hair. "Look, I'm explaining this wrong. Just promise to give me another chance to ease you into my world. Okay?"

"All right, Ben. I'd like to say that if I'd met your family weeks ago, I wouldn't have been prepared. But now we know each other better."

179

"I like how you said that. Now we're in this together. On the count of three, we'll open the door. Ready?"

When they entered the main room of the cabin, nobody took notice of them. Lexi was busy rummaging through cupboards to find cooking utensils at their mother's orders and Dylan was digging all the fishing tackle out of a closet while Sean checked the poles' rigging.

Everyone else must be outside. Coolers and bags of food littered the dock.

"How the hell'd you all fit on that old pirogue anyway? It's a wonder it didn't sink," Ben said by way of greeting.

Tyler threw him a dirty look. "Almost did. Got my foot wet." She lifted her running shoe, which looked a shade darker than the other.

Ben walked up to his little sister and put his arms around her. "I'm not teaching you how to ride that motorcycle, Tyleri."

She batted at him, nearly shoving him off the dock. He laughed but noted how her eyes zeroed in on his injuries he sported. He sobered. "Well, maybe I'll teach you."

Sweeter now, she went on tiptoe to kiss his cheek. Then Sean walked out, and Ben broke away to meet his brother. He wanted to get him alone, but he'd been at the cabin enough with his family to know that alone time was scarce. He stopped Sean with a grip on his shoulder.

"I have you to thank for getting everyone out of there safe, bro."

Sean's lips pulled tight across his teeth. "Just doin' my job."

"I know, and you're a damn good leader as well as a team member. You knew what to do, and everyone's alive because of you."

Sean's gaze dipped to the red line on Ben's throat. "Yeah," he grated out, "we're damn lucky. But all part of the job, right?"

"Yes, but your handle on tactical maneuvers is—"

Cutting across him, Sean said, "Nah, bro, my skill just complements what you bring to the team." He grasped Ben's shoulder roughly and pulled him into a bro-hug.

Their mother's voice ended the moment. "Ben, sweetheart, will you be a dear and fetch that red cooler in here for me? I need to start chopping the tomatoes for the salad."

Ben reached for the cooler. Their father had already gotten the grill fired up. Wisps of smoke curled from the charcoal and wood mixture they cooked over, and Ben's stomach growled at the idea of a big, traditional Knight meal.

With Dahlia at his side.

He stopped beside his father and stared at the flames already turning into the perfect embers for grilling.

"She's a pretty one," his father said.

Ben gave a single nod.

"Good to see ya, son. Your brothers said..."

Ben arched a brow. What happened on that mission had better remain confidential or he'd have to put on his captain pants and dole out some punishment to his team.

"Don't worry—their mouths are sealed up tight as clams. But they don't have to say much. You know that."

Affection for his father swept through Ben. He grasped his *pere's* shoulder. "I know."

His father reeled him in for a brief hug. "Damn glad you're okay."

"So am I. Now what's for grub?"

While he detailed chicken, shrimp and roasted corn, Ben glanced over at his brothers, Chaz and Roades on the dock, lines already in the water and more at ease than he'd seen them forever. Roades didn't even appear to be favoring his leg, though he wore a brace around his thigh.

Ben hadn't seen them all together since shit had gone downhill, but he pushed those memories from his mind and savored what he had right now.

* * * * *

This was a day of firsts for Dahlia. The first time she'd watched Ben in action, stalking around with a weapon in hand, looking hot as hell. And the first time she'd ever met a boyfriend's family wearing nothing but a man's T-shirt and not a stitch on underneath.

Also, the first time she'd been swept into a big family and felt she belonged.

The long plank table was set up on the dock and the breezes washed the good scents of Cajun cuisine toward her. The Knight family took up a lot of space, but Ben had made room for her to squeeze in between him and Lexi.

Dahlia watched the woman from the corner of her eye. There was something different about her, but she couldn't put her finger on it. Then Tyler was as sassy and bold as the brothers, trash-talking each in turn. Ben's parents were kind to Dahlia and kept trying to feed her by passing dish after dish her way until her plate was overflowing.

Ben just shot her a grin and talked baseball scores with his brothers. Dahlia couldn't help but sit in awe. These men fought wars and protected the country on a daily basis. They did unspeakable acts. Yet here they sat, munching on seasoned shrimp and corn like anybody else.

The cabin's surroundings were beginning to become familiar to Dahlia, as was sitting next to Ben. Just being with the man surprised her every time she thought of it. And right now, with him bumping her arm each time he raised the corn on the cob to his mouth, she could easily imagine herself being at his side forever.

Which also terrified her. One dinner with his family wasn't a marriage proposal. She had to stay in the moment, just enjoy her meal.

"Dahlia, what do you do?" his *maman* asked. She'd asked Dahlia to call her Ellietta, an odd name but in the Deep South, any name was acceptable.

She swallowed the bite of shrimp she'd taken before speaking. "I'm a 911 operator."

"Wow, that's fantastic," Lexi spoke up. "So you save people. Like Ben."

Dahlia looked up into his eyes and something passed between them, a deeper understanding of what drew them together and could possibly keep them together.

Feeling weirdly shaken, Dahlia glanced away and resumed her conversation, answering Lexi's questions and a few from Ellietta. When she couldn't pack another shrimp into her stomach, she folded her hands over her midsection.

Sean's eyes twinkled as he raised his jaw at her gesture. "You full, Dahlia? You'll have to get more game if you're going to keep up with the Knights."

It was true—each of them was packing enough food away to feed a third world village and yet they seemed to all be fit. The dishes were quickly emptying, and Ellietta had promised a peach crumble for dessert. Dahlia might not have much room, but she could get a few more bites down for peach crumble.

"Not everyone can win eating contests like you, Sean," Ben said, taking his third ear of corn.

"Eating contests?" Dahlia asked to get some of the focus off herself.

Ben chuckled. "Yeah, Sean has always been a big eater and from the age of six discovered he can pack away enough hot dogs to win a county fair."

"Which sent him to the state champs," Tyler piped up.

"How would you know? You weren't even born yet, *Tyleri*," Sean said around a bite of buttery corn.

Dahlia looked to Ben for clarification on the name Sean had called their sister.

"Tyleri is our dear sister's nickname."

"Is not," she shot back. "You asses just call me that to drive me crazy."

"Language," their *maman* chided with a hint of a smile at her grown children's antics. Dahlia could only imagine the pride the woman must feel to have raised all of these kids and made it through with all her hair.

"Well," Tyler huffed, grabbing another roll from the basket, "this is your fault, *Maman*."

Ellietta rolled her eyes. "Here we go, Chip," she said to her husband, an older but just as handsome version of Ben.

Tyler stared at Dahlia as she told the story. "My parents didn't know I was coming, and instead of taking a few more minutes or even *days* to come up with a female name for me, they gave me the boy's name they had in mind. I bided my time until I could talk—"

"Now she's hitting her speed," Ben said, to laughter.

"—and voice my disapproval," Tyler continued, waving her fork like a sword she'd use to stab anyone who interrupted again, "and when I finally told my family I hated my name because it's a boy's name, Ben and these jerks," she twitched her fork at Roades, seated on her right, "started calling me Tyleri."

"It's very feminine," Lexi said, pressing her lips together to hold back her laugh.

"And my own twin doesn't even have sympathy for me. No wonder—she's got the good name." Tyler's grumble only made the whole family chuckle.

"But think of all the things you've been able to do with a boy's name," Lexi said.

"Right, baseball, for one." Ben ran his tongue along the corn he held in front of his face, gathering the creamy butter and making Dahlia clamp her thighs shut on the memory of that tongue in other places.

"Tyler joined the boys' baseball league and stuffed her hair under her hat. By the time they realized she's a girl, she'd pitched a no-hitter."

Tyler looked a bit more appeased, but she was obviously used to getting her way in this family and was reserving her smiles for something bigger.

Dahlia liked each and every one of the family members. So far, she'd heard little from Dylan, who sat across from her looking studious in a pair of horn-rimmed glasses. And Sean seemed preoccupied with something, keeping out of most of the conversation and only occasionally speaking or offering smiles.

Or maybe it was just Dahlia's innate sense of a person's well-being from all those 911 calls she took. She might be imagining it. Though the way Ben kept glancing at Sean too, she thought he must be picking up on the vibes as well.

After the meal was finished, she stood to help clear the table, but Ben got up and pushed her back onto the bench. Tyler, Lexi and their mother all remained seated.

Ben's smile was soft and made her heart flip. "We men do the dishes. You sit and try to eat more of that peach crumble."

Her smile widened, and she watched him gather half a dozen platters in his big, capable hands and carry them inside the house.

Lexi giggled, causing Dahlia to look up in confusion.

"You have that look on your face, Dahlia."

"What look?"

187

"The look we didn't think we'd ever see on any woman's face for our brother."

"What? Ben's been with a lot of women. I'm sure many of them have looked at him in whatever way I was—or wasn't—looking."

Lexi nodded. "That's true—he's had a lot of women. But thing is, Dahlia, we've never met a single one."

The impact of what Lexi was telling her struck. Ben had never allowed his family to meet any of the women he'd been with. Sure, the Knights had barged into the cabin in the middle of their lovemaking and there had been no choice but to meet her.

But before that, he'd asked to take her home with him and show her off for himself.

Dahlia raised a bite of sweet peaches to her mouth, ducking her head to conceal the flush of pleasure in her cheeks.

Chapter Eight

Ben watched his teammate approach, searching his gait for infirmities, but Rocko had that same cocky bounce in his step he always had. Climbing off his barstool, Ben extended a hand to the guy.

"Looks like you're getting around fine, but those docs forgot to fix something."

"What's that?" Rocko kept his expression neutral as usual.

"Your face is still as ugly as ever."

Rocko nodded. "Takes an ugly fucker to know an ugly fucker. You buyin' me a drink or what?"

Ben waved at the stool next to his, and Rocko slid onto it without a wince at the movement. Good—real good. Ben needed all of them healthy and whole, because he had a gut feeling another mission would be dumped on them soon. It wouldn't surprise him to get the call right this minute.

Rocko ordered his drink and they sat sipping in silence. Last time Ben had sat at this bar, he'd been dreaming of Key West and a set of golf irons. So much had changed in such a short amount of time, and fact was, he wasn't sure how he felt about any of it.

"That's the longest you've ever kept your mouth shut." Rocko raised his drink again.

He pushed out a sigh. "Just a lot on my mind."

"Something to do with the force?"

He shifted his shoulders, his shirt suddenly feeling very tight. "I didn't sign up for this, but it was handed to me."

"Sounds like you have resentment."

Did he? He thought harder and finally shook his head. "No, that isn't it. I'm honored to be given the assignment."

"Is it because of what happened to you last time?"

The feeling of blows raining down on him and the flames licking at his skin haunted him, an echo of the past he had to shove into a closet and lock the door on, like every other man in his situation.

"No." His voice grated, and he downed the rest of his whiskey.

"Then it has to be a woman."

Swallowing the burning alcohol, he considered this new question. He'd never thought Rocko to be much of a conversationalist, but then again, they still didn't know each other well. There was a bond between them, sure, because of what they faced together. But they'd never hung out this way.

He ordered another drink and when it was in hand again, he responded to Rocko's statement.

"There is someone I need to think of. I guess it has me wondering how far she's willing to go with me."

"Like can she not hear from her man for a week, month, maybe more and live through the fear of what's happening to him?"

He nodded.

"Have you asked her?"

"I already know she grew up in a similar situation."

"Jackson," Rocko said.

"Yes."

"Then she's well aware of the lifestyle. But does she love you enough to see you through it? To wave goodbye to you and give you a pretty smile to give you something to remember when you're facing that shit we face?"

Ben's chest grew hot. "Love hasn't been discussed."

"But you love her already."

"Damn, when did you get so intuitive?"

Rocko grinned and spread his first two fingers to point to each of his eyes. "I'm not blind. Anybody who sees you look at her knows you love her."

Until that minute, he hadn't admitted it to himself, yet Rocko was right. He was in love with Dahlia and keeping her happy had rapidly become his lifelong mission, something he'd walk through the fires of hell to see completed every single day.

They drank in silence a bit longer. The clink of the bottles and glasses offered a calming atmosphere, as did Rocko's undemanding presence. He was simply Ben's friend right now, there to listen or just drink.

"Will you give it up for her?" Rocko asked after a while.

Ben set down his empty glass. "If she asks."

"Then let's hope she doesn't ask, because I heard something through the grapevine that's about to go down."

Ben stared at him. "Let's take this outside."

With a nod, Rocko knocked back his drink and they left the bar and got into Rocko's SUV.

Ben turned to him. "How the hell are you getting intel and I'm not?"

"My former team was deployed at oh-six-hundred, and I got a text from one at 5:58."

Swallowing back his adrenaline that had started pumping the minute Rocko had dropped the words back in the bar, Ben asked, "And it said?"

"See you over there, buddy."

"Over there."

Rocko nodded.

"Fuck."

"You didn't hear it from me, when Jackson finally gets around to telling us to scramble."

"'Course not." Ben rubbed at his jaw, rasping with stubble. Where the hell were they headed and into what for how long? The questions could fly at him all day like bullets in the fucking Afghan desert, but he'd know nothing until Jackson wanted him to.

He reached for the door handle.

"Where you goin'?" Rocko asked.

"If we only have a few hours, I need to be with my girl."

Rocko's teeth flashed white with his grin. "Yes, you do. See you soon, Cap'n." He gave a lazy, half-assed salute that Ben would let slide this time.

Throwing him a smile in return, he got out and closed the door. Rocko pulled out of the parking lot seconds later and Ben followed him down the road until their paths split and he headed toward the Market District.

He let himself into Dahlia's apartment and checked his watch. She still had another hour on her long shift, and he considered going over there and demanding that her boss let her go early, but that wasn't right. She had a job before him, the same as he did.

He sank to her sofa, a subtle gray that looked as hard as cement but when he stretched out, he found it was surprisingly comfortable. Even reclining, his mind was hard at work, already going over what he'd say to his men, how he needed to text his parents and sisters so they had a last conversation with him before he headed into whatever hell they were meant to face.

Drawing a throw pillow under his head, he caught a whiff of Dahlia's scent lingering on the fabric. His eyes drifted shut and his mind wandered through their time together in the cabin. Being with her alone had been incredible. But even when his family had shown up, which had thrown him for a hell of a loop, she'd gotten along with them well.

His family liked her, and Dahlia had enjoyed herself, laughing with his sisters as they all sat on the dock together long after the stars popped out. In bed that night, she'd snuggled against Ben and told him what a good day she'd had.

Dammit, he didn't want to leave her right now, when things were getting so good between them.

The sound of the key in the lock roused him, and he sat up just as Dahlia walked in. When he set eyes on her, his heart gave a happy thump, and if he hadn't already admitted his feelings back in that bar with Rocko, he sure as hell was now. Nobody had made him feel this way besides Dahlia.

She wore slim pants and a frilly white top, her hair pulled off her face in a way he hadn't seen it before.

There was so much to learn about her, and leaving would put that on hold, dammit.

What choice did he have?

She was lugging a leather purse and a huge bag stuffed with what appeared to be a blue blanket.

"Are you having naptime at the office now?" he asked, getting up to take the bag from her.

She smiled. "It's my knitting project I mentioned to you." She looked more closely at him. "What are you doing here?"

"Thought I'd surprise you. Is that all right?" He cupped her face, and she leaned into his hand, giving him another tug on the old heartstrings.

"I'm glad to see you. I had a…" Her throat worked for a second, and with alarm, he saw her eyes were red-rimmed. "I had a rough day. I'm just going to change clothes and take a second to regroup, okay?"

"Of course." He'd never seen her this way, but damn, did he know what she was going through. At times the stress was so much to bear, and those precious seconds she asked for could really help.

Leaning in, he kissed her softly. "Take the time you need. I'll just be out here."

She gave him a grateful smile and then disappeared into her room. Ben went back to the sofa and sank down, setting the knitting bag on the floor. He reached in and pulled it out, examining the even, orderly stitches that helped to keep Dahlia sane when things were going sideways. He had his own coping mechanisms. Everyone did.

He found the needles still in place and twisted the yarn around his finger. It took him a minute to find the rhythm but soon he'd worked through a dozen or so stitches.

"Ben!"

He looked up to find Dahlia standing there in sweats and an old Astros T-shirt.

"What the... Are you knitting?" She rushed across the room and plopped down on the couch to look closely at his stitches. "Oh my God, you are! How did you learn?"

A sheepish smile crossed his face and he passed her the project. "There was a guy in my platoon who did it to relax. He showed me how."

Her eyes twinkled. "I'm shocked that a big, burly Marine like you can knit. Actually, I think your stitches are better than mine. Now I'm jealous."

"Yeah? Hmm. Well, let me show you how I use my needle." He arched a brow.

With a toss of her hair, she climbed into his lap to straddle him. He planted his hands on her hips and claimed her mouth. There was no saltiness of tears, and whatever trauma she'd lived through seemed to be gone for now, and if it wasn't, he was damn well going to chase it away.

He drew her deeper into the kiss, and she clutched at his shoulders, pushing her pussy down on the bulge of his jeans. Lust pulsed through him. Groaning, he clamped her tighter to him and slanted his mouth over hers again and again.

Between long sweeps of his tongue, he said, "Dahlia, do you think you should quit your job?"

She stilled. "What?"

"I hate seeing you stressed."

She drew away to look into his eyes as if stunned he'd made such a suggestion. "Just because I have a stressful day doesn't mean I don't love my job. What I do is really important. Helping people is really important to me."

Crap, now he'd offended her.

"How else do I earn a living? Or do I just run home to daddy? He has a big house, spare rooms for me."

Ben started to shake his head, but she cut him off.

"What about all the time and training I've put in? I just throw those things away?" She settled a hand on her hip, fire flashing in her eyes.

Okay, offended her was a bit of an understatement. "I just thought there are other ways you can be just as helpful. Healthcare or —"

She was shaking her head. "You think that wouldn't be equally as stressful? Watching people die in person?" Her voice cracked, and she climbed off his lap, stepping back from the sofa and folding her arms over her chest.

Ben took in her defensive pose and had no idea how to fix his open-mouth-insert-foot moment. He stood and stepped up to her, not touching her, dying to touch her.

"I only want the best for you, honey."

"Well, your job's stressful. I see how you came back, battered and hollow-eyed after that last mission. Why don't you quit?"

He tightened his lips and she swayed back and forth to force him to meet her eyes. She had no idea of the nerve she'd struck and how close to his line of thinking she was. For the time being, he didn't need to chase after the money. He could give it all up and work some construction job, pounding concrete nine to five.

Except there was Sean to look after. Dylan, Chaz and Roades. And Rocko.

He slid his fingers through his hair. "I'm sorry I brought it up. I didn't mean to offend you. I just hate seeing you suffering after a day's work and no amount of knitting's going to ease that."

"No," she said quietly. "But you do."

An involuntary noise broke from him as he grabbed her. His mouth landed on hers and skittered off as he lifted her and tossed her over his shoulder. Her plump behind rode around his ear.

Squealing, she kicked her feet, and he delivered a sound slap to her ass.

"Ahhh! Ben!"

He smacked her lighter this time and then slipped his fingers down the cleft of her ass. He couldn't wait to strip these sweats off and have his way with her.

Each step he took to the bedroom had his cock throbbing harder. By the time he dropped her onto the bed and followed her down, blanketing her with his body, he was steely-hard.

Breathless, she stared into his eyes, her teeth set in her bottom lip.

Slowly, he gripped her wrists and stretched them over her head, pinning her with hands, his body, his stare. "I'm going to fuck you until you can't even remember your own name let alone the stress you were feeling."

Her eyelids fluttered. "Is that a dare?"

"It's a promise." He stamped her mouth with his and kept both of her wrists pinned overhead in one of his own hands as he began teasing her with light kisses. Along her lower lip, to the corner of her jaw and around to her ear. Then reaching her neck with the point of his tongue.

She bucked upward. "Stop teasing."

"Not a chance, honey." He sucked at her throat until she writhed. Moving one hand across her body, he cupped her breast and flicked the distended tip through her T-shirt and bra. Stripping her would take more time than he wanted to spend—he was too eager to bury his cock in her. But he needed to take his time and give her an overload of sensations to help her unwind.

Or unravel.

He closed his fingers over her nipple lightly at first and then increasing the pressure until she cried out.

He moved his hand, and she arched her back. "Do that again."

"Hmm. You like this?" He watched her face as he repeated the move. Seeing her face grow pink and desire flood her eyes was enough to drive a man crazy. A woman like her came around once in a lifetime, and he was damn well going to hang on.

He just prayed he could keep her.

The soft moans coming from her sweet lips had him aching to strip her immediately. Forcing himself to keep it slow, he kissed down to her breast and clamped his teeth over one nipple.

"My God, Ben," she cried.

He released her hands to pull up her T-shirt, but she didn't move them from over her head as he slowly raised the hem. Spattering her stomach with kisses and a series of short flicks of his tongue until he reached her bra. It took half a heartbeat to strip her bare, the top and bra abandoned on the floor.

She smelled of sweet perfume and sweeter arousal. He wasn't going to last long and one taste of her would make him blow.

He slid his hand into her stretchy waist of her sweats. Finding her bare.

He stopped dead, looking into her eyes. "You're not wearing any panties."

She shook her head, a glimmer of invitation in those dark eyes that had him acting.

Without pause, he sank his fingers into her tight sheath. Two fingers stretching, plunging as he sucked her nipples and she trembled under him. When he added a third finger, stretching her to the limit, she cried out.

Ben surged upward to capture her lips, still fingering her, hand moving in her sweats like they were teens on a Friday night. Except he had much more adult visions for their future, and it involved a church and him decked out in a tuxedo.

How he'd fallen for her so damn completely was anybody's guess, but right now all he could think about was getting Dahlia to scream. He tore his lips away, hovering over her as he curled his fingertips inside her pussy.

"Come for me, honey. I want you to soak my fingers."

* * * * *

A dark heat gripped Dahlia's lower belly, and she wanted that tension to draw tighter and tighter until it finally snapped like a thin cord and she did what he was demanding of her.

To come and soak his fingers.

She rocked her hips. His fingers filled her completely, and a deep thrum was beginning inside her core. One brush of his thumb over her clit and she'd be shooting like a star through the sky.

His scent enveloped her, and her mind blanked to anything but the pleasure he was giving her. Hope rose with each tick closer to the end she got. Why *couldn't* this work—them? A real relationship, with crazy-hot sex on a weeknight followed by big bowls of ice cream and her feet in his lap as they watched a movie? Free time at the cabin, loving each other to the music of the bayou. And waking in each other's arms.

He stilled his fingers, applying pressure to her inner wall. Juices flooded his hand, and he groaned. She mewled in answer and found his lips. Their mouths clung, their tongues slowed.

When he moved his fingers a fraction, it was enough. Liquid heat claimed her body, and she shook as the orgasm hit full-force. A scream left her throat, and Ben plunged his fingers in and out of her pussy in time to her pulsations as he twirled his tongue over hers.

The release only provided a moment of relief, because he withdrew his fingers and then thrust them back in harder. Mimicking what she needed from his cock.

She grabbed at him. "Ben, I need you. Now." Sliding her hands between them, she popped his jeans button and unzipped his fly. Reaching inside his briefs, she gripped his thick cock at the base and stroked the full length to the tip.

He threw his head back on a growl. "Keep that up and I won't get inside you." He rolled away and she watched him kick off his jeans and roll on a condom. She shimmied off her sweats, damp from her release. Holding his stare, she didn't think her heart could get any fuller. She couldn't fall in love with him more.

He stood there for a long minute just staring at her. When she got off the bed and wrapped her arms around him, he cupped her face with so much tenderness. "Honey, I want more of the more I asked for before. I—"

She silenced him with a kiss, going on tiptoe and hooking her calf around his tree trunk of a leg.

Groaning, he lifted her in one fluid move, tucking her thighs around his waist and easing her down on his cock. Each inch that filled her had her crying out louder. Holding her under the ass, he began to move. Rocking his hips as she slid up and down on him, her nipples rubbing against his hard chest and the head of his cock stretching her soooo deep.

What had he been about to say to her and why had she cut him off?

Because empty promises and meaningless words of love weren't things she wanted to hear. She was in the present, enjoying this sexy Marine with every cell of her being, and that was enough.

Wasn't it?

In her mind's eye, the fantasy about the cabin had included some little Knight children running around on the dock, catching fish and exclaiming over the gators. But no, Dahlia wasn't thinking on them. They'd never exist.

She clung to his neck as she slid up and down on his long cock, taking every inch of Ben. Need splintered through her, and she cried out for a second time.

Ben's muscles strained, and the cords in his neck stood out sharply as he turned for the bed once more. Laying her down gently and standing at the side of the bed to thrust into her with hard jerks that reached deep into her body — and soul.

"Look at me, honey." His gritty tone drew her gaze to his. Their eyes locked. Desire and another emotion pooled together, mingling into a bond that could only end in disaster.

She freakin' loved him. Loved a walking ghost. How long before something happened and she was left a widow, possibly with those happy little kids on the dock?

"Don't look away. Right here." He fucked her with a slowness that was nothing but deliberate. With a shock, she realized he was *trying* to claim her in all ways — body, mind and soul.

"Ben." Her voice shook.

"This is happening, honey. Don't fight it."

As soon as his words washed through her brain, her body seemed to surrender to him, and she was helpless to fight the pull of this man.

* * * * *

"If you put the needles at a bit more of an angle, you'll get a tighter stitch." Ben demonstrated with a couple stitches, the blue yarn sliding through his fingers.

She stared at him in amazement.

"What?" He suddenly felt a bit self-conscious, and that never happened.

"I never guessed this of you, Ben. That you have a softer side."

"Well. Now I feel like doing something really manly like going to the shooting range or something. But yeah, it's part of me."

"What else don't I know?" She stretched out on her side with her head propped on her hand.

He set aside the needles and did the same. "I don't crochet."

"Damn." She grinned.

"Or sew, though any Marine worth his ass will know how to affix a button."

"I'll remember to come to you then. I'm hopeless with those things."

He reached out and stroked her hair off her cheek. "What about your father? How will he feel about us?"

She groaned. "He's resistant but he knows what you are and who you are. And in the end, it's my choice. Why are you grinning like that?"

"Am I grinning?"

"Like a crazy man, yes."

"I guess I love thinking of you choosing me. And telling your father where to stick it."

"You mean telling the colonel where to stick it."

"Something like that."

She chuckled. "Tell me about your parents. Did I pass the test?"

"Honey, there was never a test. They loved you. My siblings too, especially Lexi. I think she's excited to have someone new in her life."

"I really enjoyed talking with her."

"I keep asking my brothers what they did to that boyfriend of hers, but they refuse to tell me." During their alone time in the cabin, Ben had filled her in about everything including why they were all so protective of their sister. She couldn't blame them, though Lexi seemed very capable of handling herself in almost all ways.

"What about the team?" she asked him, studying the small frown that had appeared between his brows at the mention of his sister's trouble.

His gaze cleared. "What about them?"

"I know a team is like a brotherhood."

He laughed. "They *are* my brothers."

"I know. But they're more than that, and I just wondered if they like me."

"What does it matter if they don't?"

"Because I'm guessing I'll see a lot more of them if I'm in your life."

His eyes warmed as he slowly leaned in to brush a kiss across her lips. "They love you and will protect you like their own family, just as they protect me."

She shook her head. "That's not what I was expecting, and I hope I never need protecting. But I can't deny that I like the perks of being with a Knight."

"Mmm. I can think of a few more perks. Wanna learn about them?"

"Uh-huh." She nibbled at his lower lip, raising a growl. Then he was flipping her, tumbling her to the mattress and showing her things she never imagined.

* * * * *

Ben knew the second Dahlia realized what he had hours earlier. He saw that glimmer of worry in her eyes, followed by joy and finally sweet surrender.

"I can't get close enough." He jerked his cock into her, bottoming out, and leaned over her to steal more long kisses. This wasn't mindless fucking—it was deliberate lovemaking with a woman he planned to be with for the rest of his life.

He flipped his tongue against hers and bottomed out again. She gasped, and he repeated the move. Each clench of her tight channel around him had his balls tightening, about to explode. When he did, he'd be lucky to remain conscious — or keep from spouting his love for her and scaring her off.

He lifted her ass off the mattress as he slammed her. "Come on, honey. Feel my cock so deep, rubbing your pussy right... there." He thrust again.

She threw her head back, eyes sealed shut with bliss.

The beauty of her expression, her plump lips, her breasts jiggling... all melded until he couldn't hold back anymore.

Pumping into her body, aware of the tiny flutters dancing around his cock as her own release struck.

When his final spurt left him, his strength seemed to cave in and he collapsed atop her.

The apartment was silent all but for the tick of a clock in another room and the occasional bump on the ceiling from the neighbor above.

"Stay tonight," she whispered.

He nodded. "I'm not going anywhere." He crawled up the bed with her in tow, laying them on the pillows and within reach of the covers. Sweat dried on his body as his heartbeat slowed.

She pressed a soft kiss to his pec, followed by a flick of her tongue across his nipple.

He groaned. "Damn, woman. Already?"

"Well, you've got all this to tease a woman." She skated her hand over his chest to his carved abs.

He gave her a crooked smile. "Let's order takeout for dinner and make it an all-nighter." Or until Jackson rallied the team for deployment—whichever came first. Ben was living for the moment, unwilling to think too far into the future, and he damn well wasn't letting go of Dahlia until someone ordered him out of her bed.

The smile that spread over her beautiful features made his heart squeeze with so much love he couldn't yet voice. He brushed her silky hair off her high cheekbone.

But he would—soon.

Chapter Nine

Dahlia scooped up a bowl of ice cream in each hand and walked into the living room. Her gaze fell on the empty sofa and her heart skipped a beat. A weak, boneless feeling washed through her, and she nearly dropped the ice cream.

He'd left again. After half a night of amazing sex and cuddling through a few episodes of a Netflix series, not to mention all those sweet words Ben had given her, the asshole had walked out again.

A sound made her turn to the window, and her heart launched into her throat the sight of the rugged man standing there staring out on the dark street below. Fully dressed.

When he pivoted, she shook her head, taking a step back, the ice cream in her hands forgotten.

"I have to go, honey. I've been summoned." His lips were a tight slash, but his eyes...

Oh God.

He stepped toward her. She shook her head again. "Not now," she managed.

He crossed the space and took the bowls from her hands, setting them on the coffee table. "I'm sorry, honey. My team's waiting for me outside already."

If she was still holding the glassware, she would have rifled the bowls at the wall. Dammit, she and Ben were just finding a rhythm and once again he'd be torn from her, for how long this time? A week, a month, a year?

Her legs gave out and she dropped into a chair and dipped her head into her hands.

Ben sank to his knees before her and took her by the shoulders. "This isn't ideal timing. It never is." He gave a harsh laugh. "Just... know that I care about you so much. I—"

She searched his eyes.

"Oh fuck it. I love you, Dahlia. And I'm coming back and marrying you."

Her jaw dropped.

He tugged her against his hard chest, smashing her cheek to his shirt. "I'm so sorry it has to be now, honey. But I'll be back to make good on that promise with a ring and a personalized instruction on creating the best knitting stitches."

A laugh-sob escaped her, but her mind was whirling. Marry her?

He crushed her to him and then released her and stood, dragging her to a stand with him. Knuckling her chin up, he lowered his head and dropped a kiss of goodbye across her lips. Then withdrawing, he looked into her eyes. "I'll be back."

She watched him walk to the door and open it before her mind caught up to what was happening—

that he was leaving and she may never see him again. She ran across the room and threw herself at him.

He caught her and clutched her by the nape and if it wasn't her imagination, she felt a shiver run through him. His phone buzzed, and he released her. With a crooked smile and a wink, he walked out.

She rushed to the window trying to see him as he climbed into the waiting vehicle, but she couldn't see much more than the dim halo of light on the corner where the streetlight stood.

Spinning from the window, she dropped her head into her hands again. What the hell had just happened? On the coffee table, the ice cream melted in the bowls. Her body still tingled from Ben's very hot, very thorough lovemaking, and she was doused in his delicious male scent.

But he was gone.

Dammit, this was exactly the thing she hadn't wanted in her life. Growing up with a father who couldn't disclose his whereabouts was bad enough, and now this? This was... unfathomable.

How was she supposed to even think knowing he was out there in danger?

He'd told her he loved her, was going to marry her. And she'd stood there like a statue and said nothing.

"I love him," she whispered to the empty room.

She ran forward and snatched up her cell, punching his number he'd given her earlier. It rang once, twice, three times. Then it made an odd clicking noise that wasn't the voicemail.

His phone was already shut down, out of service, maybe flung into the Gulf for all she knew. She had no way of reaching Ben and telling him that she loved him too and would wait for him.

No, not just wait. She wanted to tell him that when he returned, she'd be ready to say I do.

* * * * *

Dahlia let herself into her father's house and closed the door behind her. The place was empty and that was exactly what she needed to break into her daddy's office and rifle his computer for records of Knight Ops' whereabouts.

She passed the sweeping staircase she'd walked down on her sweet sixteenth to a crowd of smiling friends. And she'd always envisioned herself coming down these stairs to her groom on her wedding day. But not now. After three weeks without word from her lover, she had no idea if she'd ever see him again.

Her father's office was dark with wood walls and bookcases, his big mahogany desk as old as the house it resided in and rumored to have belonged to a Civil War general.

She strode across the Chinese carpet and slipped behind the desk and into her father's leather seat. The masculine notes of the space made her heart beat out of time—if her father came home and found her trying to crack information from his system, there'd be hell to pay.

Cool air from the wall vent was useless in drying up her perspiration. Her neck felt clammy and her underarms would need a hosing down after this mission.

She signed into her father's computer, and to her bone-melting relief, it took the password. She smiled to herself—her daddy wasn't very good at keeping things from her.

Logging on to the central Homeland security system was more difficult, and after her first failed attempt, her stress hit the pinnacle. She knew there were only two attempts allowed before the government locked her out.

Dammit, what she needed was a hacker like Dylan. He'd hacked the Pentagon, for God's sake. He could surely get her in. Then again, if she had Dylan on hand, she'd have Ben and wouldn't need Dylan's services at all.

"Shit," she muttered, wracking her brain for the key code. Even if she got it right this time, there were more gates to walk through, and she wouldn't be surprised if there was a retinal scan involved.

No, she just had to think clearly.

Drawing a deep breath, she poised her fingers over the keys. Tapping out a letter, then a number. Pulse hammering in her temples.

A step in the corridor made her leap but not quick enough.

Her father, Colonel Jackson of the United States Marines and the man with the record of most scowls directed his daughter's direction, opened the office door and leveled his stare at her.

"Internet shopping, dear?"

She gulped. "There's a sale at Nordstrom. I thought I'd get a new summer dress for the party I'm throwing you."

He arched a brow and circled the desk. She didn't have a second to even close out of the screens. Her father glared at her and then leaned over and tapped a key, shutting down the entire system. He folded his arms over his chest and stared down at her.

"Want to explain yourself?"

She released a harsh breath. She wasn't afraid of him—only of what he'd say if he found out she was looking for Ben. Because she loved him.

But she was a grown woman, and she didn't need anybody, let alone her daddy, dictating her love life.

She squared her shoulders and stood to face her father. "I was looking for Ben."

His eyes flickered with something she didn't understand. "You won't find him there."

"How can I find him then?" Desperation threatened to seep into her tone, but she wasn't a child and was far from weak, so she bit back the emotion.

Her father straightened from the desk and rounded the front. He folded his hands behind his back and took off pacing.

Dahlia gripped the edge of the desk for support. As a child, she'd seen her father do this a lot when thinking. But she hadn't seen it since that day he'd called her into his office to tell her that her mother wasn't coming home from the hospital.

The blood drained from her, and she swayed. "Oh God."

Her father stopped his mid-rotation and stared at her. "Dahlia, you look about to faint. Sit down." He moved to help her into the seat again.

Tears prickled her eyes. "It's Ben, isn't it? Something happened, and this time he isn't just injured." She couldn't force out the words on her tongue and stomping all over her heart.

"Dammit, I knew that dickhead was messing around with you. I didn't know it was this far advanced, though."

Her heart convulsed. He wouldn't be calling a dead man names, especially one who'd lost his life in the name of freedom. Did that mean...?

Her father gentled his expression in a way only she and her mother had ever seen. "Dahlia, he's not dead. Not even missing in action, though I might see what can be arranged —"

"Daddy!"

"No, I don't mean that. I'm sorry. Ben's a fine Marine, the best actually. And he's done much better than we anticipated."

"What does that mean?" The blood was rapidly returning to her fingertips, leaving them tingling.

"You know I shouldn't be telling you anything, but I can't have you looking so distressed. You know, your mother had that same expression in her eyes when I'd go away every single time."

"Just tell me what's going on!"

Her father perched on the edge of the desk near her. "Ben led the team into some pretty heroic shit and even when things went bad, he pulled them out. As a result, OFFSUS is sending them out of the country again."

She shook her head, unable to ingest this. "Again? Where?"

"I can't say. But I can tell you where he's being deployed from."

She shot to her feet and grabbed her father by the shoulders, shaking him and leaning in to plant a kiss to his shaven cheek at the same time. "Thank you! Tell me please."

* * * * *

Minutes later, Dahlia had a flight booked and a call in to the Knight household. Her hands were shaking so bad, she could barely hold the phone still

217

to speak let alone drive, which was the purpose of her call.

She stood in her father's drive, tapping her feet and pacing as she waited for Ben's sisters to come to her aid.

When she spotted the blue compact car, she gave a cry and ran toward the vehicle. Tyler came to a stop and she jumped into the back seat. "Thank you guys so much for coming for me. I'm such a wreck—I've never been this wrecked even during the worst 911 calls. And there's no way I could drive myself to the airport."

Tyler twisted in the driver's seat, flashing a grin that was so like Ben's that Dahlia's heart began to pound. "We got you, girl. Hang on. I'm backing out."

When Tyler said backing out, she meant whipping the car in a half-donut in the driveway and stomping the pedal to the floor as they hit the road. In the passenger's seat, Lexi squealed with delight.

Dahlia wondered how many of these adventures the pair of them went on for their brothers' sakes. She sat back and strapped herself in, not totally trusting Tyler's driving, though she seemed to have some damn good training in keeping it on four wheels when they should be on two.

They careened around a bend and Lexi threw Dahlia a grin over her shoulder. "This is like Thelma and Louise and... *Tyleri.*"

"I just had my nails done, but I'm not so girly that I won't punch you, Lex."

Lexi just laughed. "You're not the only girl in the family who knows how to fight. Our brothers taught me too."

Not rising to the taunt or removing her eyes from the road, Tyler hit another bend at a speed that had Dahlia's stomach rolling and her eyes slamming shut on the trees and curve signs rushing past the back windows. If she made it to Ben alive, it would be a miracle.

Lexi bounced to sit sideways so she could look at Dahlia. "You look a little green. She looks green, sis. Slow down."

"No, don't slow down," Dahlia said. "I can't miss this flight."

Lexi seemed to take that as a challenge, hit a straight stretch and stomped her little—wait, was that gator skin?—boot into the pedal. They hit a three-figure speed, and Dahlia thought she might puke. But losing out on this chance to make it to Ben before he left the States was the only thing she was concerned about right now.

"Are you going to marry our brother?" Lexi asked, smile wide. "It would be great to have you as a sister-in-law. Our family loves you."

"They do?" Her stomach roiled, and she wasn't sure anymore if she was going to puke or rejoice that the Knights were on her side as well as her own stubborn, controlling father.

Lexi popped the glove compartment and rifled through half a dozen cell phones. "What does Dylan need all these phones for anyway? Oh, here it is." She extracted a plastic-coated bag and passed it to Dahlia.

"You know what our brother does with those phones. He blows shit up remotely," Tyler said.

"Puke in the bag, sweetie," Lexi said kindly.

She gulped as they careened around another corner, barely clinging to the pavement. Vehicles dodged from their path. "No," she panted, "I'm not going to puke." At least not until she was in the air and on her way to Ben.

"When y'all get back to Louisiana, we'll celebrate at the cabin. We'll make gumbo. You've never had anything as good as *Maman's* gumbo. Won't that be fun, Dahlia?" Lexi pressed on. The woman was as crazy as the rest of the Knights. How could she even talk about food when the car was moving like a paper airplaine shooting through outer space?

Probably used to it.

She pictured Tyler racing to church or the shopping center and nearly giggled. But the exit ramp for the airport loomed ahead, and Dahlia latched onto that with everything in her being.

She was nearly there. Thanks to Ben's sisters, she was going to make this flight.

Tyler took the ramp at high speed—big surprise—and skidded to a stop in front of the building. "Your destination, Ms. Jackson," she drawled with all the honey of a Southern belle—who could handle a car like a stunt driver and still rock a French manicure.

Dahlia quickly released her seatbelt, firmly swallowing her stomach again, and leaned over the seat to kiss each of his sisters' cheeks. "Thank you both! I owe you!" Then she launched from the back seat, hitting the ground running.

* * * * *

"You don't want any of this food, man? I've never seen a spread like this," Sean said.

Ben grunted. "Because it's a last supper," he muttered under his breath.

Food containers littered the glossy dining room table in the ritzy New York City suite OFFSUS had put them up in while they waited for the second they would be called to action.

"These ribs are freakin' amazing. They rival the ones at Anatole's. Try one," Sean said.

He pierced his brother with a look. "How can you even eat knowing what we're going into?"

His brother lifted a shoulder and let it fall. "Going on an empty stomach sucks even worse, don't ya think?" When Ben didn't reply, he dug into his ribs again.

The other team members sprawled over couches and the game was on the big screen. To anyone on the outside, it appeared that six buddies were living it up in the city. But Ben's guts were clenched in fear.

Not fear of gunfire or battle—that was normal for him. But fear of never returning to keep his promise to get down on one knee and ask for the hand of the woman he loved. She had to be going insane with not knowing where he was. And that look on her face as he'd walked out the door had haunted him hourly since leaving her.

He pushed out a breath. "Gimme one of those ribs."

Sean grinned, mouth greasy with barbecue, and passed the box to Ben. He fished out a rib and bit into it.

The knock at the door had them all dropping their food and launching to their feet. He snagged a napkin and wiped the sauce from his fingers as he strode to the door. When he whipped it open, he expected to come face-to-face with some man in uniform or even a man in black with black shades, here to inform them it was time.

He blinked at the person standing before him.

Dahlia's chest heaved, bringing her cleavage up against the V-neck of her top. Her hair was knotted on the back of her head and she looked like she'd shed some tears to get here, judging by the shadowed streaks beneath each beautiful eye.

But she was here, in the flesh. How the hell had she found him?

"My God." He scooped her up at the same moment she hurled herself into his arms. The impact of her body hitting his was the most bittersweet moment of his entire life.

And one he couldn't live with again.

"What are you doing here? Honey, you shouldn't have come."

"I had to see you before you go."

"You… know where we're headed?" He leaned away long enough to study her face.

She shook her head. "Not exactly. But I got the information from my father and then I had your sisters come for me. Damn, Tyler is a freakin' maniac behind the wheel, isn't she?"

Chuckles sounded from his brothers behind him, where they were looking on.

"Slow down. Honey, I need to talk to you. Alone." He glanced over his shoulder at the guys who didn't seem eager to get out and give them privacy. With a growl, he towed her through the room and into the bathroom, locking the door behind them.

She stared at him, her heart in her eyes.

All the more reason to say what he had to say— right now.

"Ben, I love you," she said at the same time he said, "I quit Knight Ops.

Her eyes widened. His chest flooded with warmth at her words.

"Are you serious?" they said together.

"Wait—you first. The loving you part can wait." She cupped his jaw.

"No, it can't. That's my point. I have to quit to be with you. To show you every day how much I love you, Dahlia."

She shook her head. "You're just going to give up what you do for me?"

"Yes."

"I-I don't need that. I wasn't sure I was willing to live this sort of life of a military wife, but I've done a lot of thinking since you've been gone—and especially on that flight here. I love you, Ben, and nothing's going to change that."

He leaned against the marble sink top. "Things always change after a mission. *I* change. I never come back the same man, honey." His voice sounded with all the weariness he felt.

She shook her head, making the knot of hair wobble. She had two sticks shoved through her hair to hold the style in place, and what he wouldn't give to pluck those free and see all her dark hair slide down into his waiting hands as he lowered his mouth to kiss her.

Every day for the rest of his life.

"I can't risk losing you. Each time I come back from whatever hell we've been through, how can I know you'll be able to still love me?"

She made a rough noise in her throat and stepped up to loop her arms around his neck. "Because that's what love is about, Ben. Each time you come home to me, I learn about all the little idiocies you gained while away."

"Don't you mean idiosyncrasies?"

She grinned, making his heart turn over.

He plastered her to his chest and swayed as he embraced her. Breathing the scent of her hair, feeling not only how soft she was against him but how giving she was.

How perfect.

"Are you sure, honey?"

"Are you sure you can walk away from your duty as captain and leave your brothers and friend to do this alone?"

He looked down into her eyes, burning with emotion. "Say the love part again."

Her smile spread. "I love you, Ben. And yes, I'll marry you. The minute you hit American soil again, I'll be waiting with my wedding gown."

He hitched her against him, wishing he could wrap his arms around her twice and hold her closer. How he deserved this woman was the biggest question of all, but not one he was willing to ask twice. She belonged to him.

"My God, I don't know how I ever found someone who was made for me."

She went on tiptoe, her lips deliciously close. She moved his hand up to cup her breast. "Let's see just how made for each other we are."

"Right here in the bathroom?"

"It's half as big as the bedroom in my apartment, so yeah. Plus, these mirrors will let me see your body from so... many... angles." She flicked her tongue over his lips with each word.

Ben couldn't waste another second. He had no idea what would be his last.

He slammed his lips over hers.

* * * * *

A deep heat pooled in Dahlia's body, but the wild urgency inside her urged Ben on. The sooner he joined their bodies, the sooner they could reach that explosive ending — then start all over.

They might have hours, minutes or seconds. And Dahlia was making the most of each moment she had with the man she loved.

He stripped off her clothes with lightning speed. With his palm on her breast and his fingers working her fly, he swallowed her soft cries of bliss on his tongue. The forbidden tone of their coupling — with the rest of Knight Ops just separated by a few walls was sexy enough. But add in the fact they were having reunion sex *and* farewell sex, and neither of them had a glimmer of control.

She had him bared to the waist, and in the mirrors her red nail marks on his shoulders were evident. She had an urge to draw blood and give him something to carry with him after he left. But she settled for sucking on his neck instead.

"Fuck, you're so wet," he murmured between rough kisses as he found what he wanted.

"I need you inside me. Don't make me wait, Ben." She didn't need to say they might not have time, because he knew it.

He rocked back, gaze piercing her as he undid his fly and drew his long, thick erection from his cargo pants. She moaned at the sight of that mushroomed head just begging for her lips and tongue.

She started to slide off the counter, but he held her in place. "As much as I want your pretty mouth all over my cock, I want inside you more."

Their gazes held as he moved toward her. "I don't have a condom."

"I don't care. I'll take my chances on a baby."

He froze. "Jesus," he said after a heartbeat. "A little Knight. Fuck." Without hesitation, he yanked her to the edge of the counter, braced a hand on her lower back and rammed his cock home.

She found a laugh escaping and threw her head back with utter joy. "I take it that means you won't mind if you make a baby right here on this countertop."

"Not a fucking bit," he grated out as he churned his hips, the head of his cock reaching so deep inside her. Her inner walls clenched at him, and she located his hard nipple with her fingertips, strumming it in time to his thrusts.

He groaned and angled his head to kiss her more passionately. The small bottle of hand soap on the counter toppled over and both ignored it, too lost in their need to give a damn if anybody in the other room heard them. Most likely, they knew what they were doing.

Dahlia ran her tongue along Ben's lower lip, and he issued a growl. "I love when you do that, honey."

"I love..." she broke off as he bumped a spot that would send her sailing in seconds. Then again.

"I feel you squeezing me. God, I'm gonna blow." He drew her tighter into his embrace as he found her erogenous zone and made it his personal quest to drive her crazy.

His reflection of tanned muscle, all chiseled sinew, had her excitement peaking. Uncontrollable noises escaped her, and Ben slammed his mouth over hers, stealing all thought. Sensation tripled, and her insides gave one hard squeeze around his thick length. She stopped breathing and closed her eyes as a wave of release overtook her.

Trembling with the force, she tried to open her eyes and see Ben's face as he stiffened and bowed in her arms. The first spurts of his cum hitting her bare inner walls shocked her. She wrapped herself around him as they rode out their ecstasy.

She collapsed against him. From the other room, a loud male cheer went up as the Knight Ops team acknowledged their finish too.

"Oh God." She twisted her face against Ben's chest, a heated flush crawling into her cheeks.

Ben chuckled. "Assholes." Affection rang in his tone.

Dahlia's heart overflowed with love as she studied his rugged features.

"*Cher*... Don't look at me that way. I promise I'll make it back to you safe."

She cradled his jaw and gazed into his eyes. "Damn right you will, Ben Knight. And I'll be waiting."

"Keep working on those new knitting stitches I showed you."

A teary chuckle left her as tears began to drip from her lashes. "I will."

"And go to my family. My parents and sisters will welcome you. There's no need for you to sit alone all the time, especially when you're stressed after work."

A small shudder ran through Dahlia. "I will, but I don't relish the idea of getting into a car again with Tyler behind the wheel."

He snorted. "She's a handful, for sure. And Lexi is far too intuitive for her own good."

"I think I found that out as well."

He arched a brow but didn't ask more. Then he let his gaze dip over her breasts, leering like a hungry dog spying a juicy steak. "When I come back, I'm putting a ring on your finger."

"You better. I might be pregnant."

"Hmmm. Better increase our odds." He pushed his still-hard cock into her pussy again, dragging a moan from her. When he withdrew, arousal flooded her all over again.

"Hurry. We may not have much time, Knight." She leaned up to nip his lower lip.

Eyes dark with wanting, he lowered his lips until they were a breath from hers. "We have forever, honey. But right now, I'm going to make you feel... soooo... good." He rocked his hips with each word, and Dahlia threw herself into the moment, living every heartbeat she shared with her lover to the fullest.

THE END

Read on for a sneak peek of HEAT OF THE KNIGHT, book 2 of Knight Ops coming soon!

Heat of the Knight

by

Em Petrova

Chapter 1

"This SOB is fast." Ben's words filled Sean's earpiece and ratcheted his heartrate up five notches.

Missing out on a foot chase when you were late to join your special ops unit was frowned upon in the military. And when the commander was your big brother, the outcome was even worse. He was in for a world of shit for this, and all for a woman.

"Heading east. I have the agent in sight. Keep your heads on a swivel." Ben's update was followed by several grunts of agreement from the rest of the team.

Sean slammed the pedal of his old El Camino to the floor and gunned it through the New Orleans streets. The city was quieter at this hour, unusual in this area. He didn't like it—his sixth sense was blaring like an alarm to scramble the troops for a strike.

"C'mon," he urged his baby, smoothing his hand over the leather steering wheel. Not half an hour before, he'd been stroking a woman into peak after peak. Getting that summons was the kiss of death for a relationship, and this was the second time he'd walked out on some very dirty bedroom play with Alisha.

While throwing on clothes and jumping behind the wheel, he never thought the Knight Ops team would be able to locate a Russian spy who'd evaded captivity for a decade. Yet they'd found him in their own back yard and had eyes on him.

"Heading northeast now. Past Creole Joe's." Ben's words came in his normal voice, and the only sign Sean had that he was sprinting was the small hiccup of air between words.

Sean took in his surroundings. Creole Joe's was a few blocks over, and he could head the Russian off.

Without bothering with turn signals, he took a bend at top speed. His left front tire rolled up over the curb but came down smoothly, barely jarring him. He ran a hand over the steering wheel, giving it the caress of affection it deserved. His car might be circa '78 but it outperformed many modern models. And looked cool as hell.

"Closing the gap. Ninja, you got him in view?" Ben asked.

A laugh sounded. "Since when are you calling me Ninja?" their youngest brother Roades asked.

"Quit fucking around and answer the question, dickhead."

Another laugh from Roades. "The agent is not in sight, Captain."

"Dammit. You and Dylan must be off course."

"We're not off course," Dylan put in. "We know these streets like we know our own dicks, sir."

More laughter from the other guys, who were fanned across the five-block area, by the sounds of it. Still, Sean was the closest. And he had a six-cylinder.

A flash of something caught his eye and he veered left just as the man they were chasing hurdled a fire hydrant feet away from Sean. He screeched to a stop and threw the car in park, hitting the ground running. The Russian might be fast, but so was he.

Pumping his arms close to his body to generate speed, he gained on the man. The guy threw a wild look over his shoulder, and in that second Sean knew he'd do anything to escape. He was a wild animal, cornered by the people who'd ship him to his mother country, where he'd be looked in the eyes before being shot for letting down his commanders. If he stayed in the US, he'd only find himself imprisoned for life under top security.

He threw himself forward and hit the man from behind, launching them both onto the pavement. The air hung with the scent of yeast from the nearby bakery, but Sean's nose flooded with the reek of sweat and fear.

"Don't fucking move," he growled as he whipped the man's wrists together, and with one jerk of his hand, bound them with a zip-tie the Knight Ops preferred.

"You got me out of bed with a very beautiful woman, asshole, and I'm not going to go easy on you," he said to the man glaring up at him from one eye. He tightened the tie until the flesh swelled around the plastic—he couldn't risk the guy getting free.

"I got him on the ground," he said to his team.

"What the fuck? Thunder?" His brother Chaz sounded stunned.

"No, it's Santa Clause. Did you assholes think I'd abandon you?" He kept a knee in the man's back. "Name," he demanded.

"Fuck off." Damn, the guy's English was better than his own. No wonder he'd managed to fit in undetected among the Americans for a decade.

Using only a portion of his strength, Sean hauled the man to his feet. "Walk nicely now. I don't want to have to take out my weapon. Then again, you did fuck up a very enjoyable experience."

When the man didn't budge, Sean kicked his Achilles. The Russian groaned and slowly trundled forward.

Sean led the criminal to the back of the El Camino and depressed a button to raise the tonneau cover over the truck bed. The cover lifted, revealing a tool box big enough to fit a man.

The Russian tensed. "You don't plan to put me in there, do you?"

He looked over the Russian's physique. Yeah, he'd fit, no problem.

Sean contemplated the scars on his face, probably put there by the people he'd failed. Yet there were

236

more open areas of skin than scars, which meant he'd had a successful career. Now it was at an end.

"Yes, I fucking do intend to put you in there. Did you think you were getting a cushy ride to the airport?" He dragged the man a few more inches to the back of the vehicle and pushed up the lid of the toolbox. "See? Lots of space. Breathing room, we'll call it. Except you'll be gagged." He one-handedly removed a bandana from his back pocket, ignoring the faint whiff of perfume clinging to the fibers.

"Smells like a cheap whore," the Russian spat before Sean stuffed it in his mouth.

He glared at the spy, who stood two inches shorter. "Not nice to talk about a lady like that. Now get in the box."

He stood there unmoving just as Ben and Chaz careened around the corner and skidded to a stop by the El Camino.

"Now it's three against one. I know you don't like those odds. Get in the box." Sean's voice grated with authority.

Ben and Chaz closed in, reaching for the Russian. Chaz used a short bungee cord around his mouth to hold in the bandana Sean had stuffed inside. Then the two lifted him bodily and dropped him into the box.

Sean stared at the man impassively. In the past few months he'd been part of Operation Freedom Flag Southern US division, or OFFSUS, he'd seen and done some wild shit, but this guy deserved far worse than transport in his toolbox.

Sean moved to close the lid, but the man kept his ankle on the edge. "Move it or I'll smash it. We weren't told to deliver you whole—just alive."

So much hate burned from the man's eyes as Sean bound his feet as well.

"You never told me your name," Sean said in a deadly, low Russian with a perfect accent. The guy's eyes widened minutely at Sean's use of his native tongue. "But you don't need to. Say goodnight, Aleksandr Polakoff."

He slammed the lid and turned to his brothers and fellow teammates.

Ben raked his fingers through his hair. "Jesus, Sean."

Without a word, Sean circled to the driver's side and got behind the wheel. Through the open window, he heard Ben giving Chaz orders to meet up with the rest of the team and follow. Then Ben slid in, riding shotgun.

Sean pulled into the street.

"Where the hell have you been?" Ben demanded.

"Occupied. Won't happen again, Captain." He really did feel damn bad that Knight Ops had begun this mission without him, solely because he couldn't untie Alisha, make sure she was okay, dress and arrive in time.

"Damn straight you will or I'll have you court martialed and shot." Ben's tone was the no-nonsense bark of a captain, not a big brother. And Sean couldn't blame him. The team's success and safety depended on them all doing their jobs.

"I know it's all bluff." Sean shot him a sidelong look.

Ben didn't glance away from the windshield. "Try me."

Silence descended as they rolled through the Louisiana streets, the lights of businesses switched off and leaving only shadowed storefronts.

"Why the hell was Polakoff in the Big Easy anyway?" Sean asked after a spell.

"Who the hell knows. Must be meeting someone."

"Who tipped off OFFSUS?"

Ben lifted a shoulder and let it fall. The action could be a shrug or Ben's signature move when he felt uncomfortable about answering a question. Not unusual in the Knight family, considering their positions.

"Guess we'll hear it all when we debrief."

"Yeah." Ben sat silent for another block or two. Finally, he said, "So how tall was she?"

Sean grinned. "A gentleman never talks." His mind was thick with images of the sultry Alisha, long-limbed and strung up, about to be seduced out of her pretty little mind. He'd been seeing her for a month or so, and to say their nights were hot was like calling a Marine a wimp.

"You bringing her to the cabin this weekend?"

Now it was time for Sean to shift his shoulders in a semblance of an uncommitted shrug. Though he'd been considering taking Alisha to the family cabin to meet his *maman* and *pere*, he wasn't sure they were at that level yet. Besides, Knights were playboys.

"I've thought about bringing her," he said finally. "If we're actually at the cabin, that is." The Knight brothers were first and foremost defenders of their country. While based in the South, they'd found themselves flown off the grid, gaining more notoriety than Seal Team 6 the past few months.

"Yeah, might not be good idea to bring her just yet."

Sean nodded, eyes directed on the road leading to the base where they'd unload the baggage in the back.

"You did good back there, Sean. But you know I have to tell Jackson that you were late to the scene."

He grunted. "Second in command's usually the fuck-up, so he'll be expecting it."

The gates opened, and he rolled through, followed by the black SUV driven by the rest of the team. The next hours consisted of every word of the story coming out. When Colonel Jackson got Sean alone, the intimidating officer gave him the cold stare that typically made a Marine's gonads crawl inside and seek shelter.

Standing at attention, Sean stared back.

"At ease, Knight. I hear you were late to the party."

"With all respect, sir, I *was* the party. I captured Polakoff."

He narrowed his eyes at Sean. "You Knight brothers are all the same—mouthy. Your parents raise you to be mouthy, Knight?"

"No, sir. Had my mouth washed out with soap more days than I can count."

Colonel Jackson grunted. "That El Camino's pretty damn good for hauling prisoners."

He grinned. "Yes, sir."

Long seconds passed. Sean had been sized up many times in his lifetime, and he knew when a man was assessing him. Colonel Jackson was damn good at making a Marine shake in his boots, if Sean was the boot-shaking type.

"What do you want for yourself, Knight?"

He blinked. "Sir?"

"What are your goals? And you better not give me that bullshit Ben did when he said he wanted to golf, fish and fuck."

Sean smirked. "I love me some catfishin', sir. Can't deny it." His Cajun drawl was even more pronounced when talking about the things he loved.

"Catfishin'. Hmm. I'd say you love hunting the ladies too." He gave Sean's shoulder a sniff. "Do you have aspirations of your own team someday?"

He jolted. "My own team?"

"Leading your own team. Taking control."

Mind whirling, Sean wondered if the colonel had learned to dig into a man's psyche or if he was in this superior position because he knew how to do it. Since his second tour, Sean had thought of pushing for that top spot in the food chain, but since being recruited to OFFSUS, he hadn't given it much thought.

"You're damn good at strategy, Knight."

"Thank you, sir."

"There might be something opening up for you in the months to come. Be sure your tardiness doesn't hamper that. Dismissed."

Sean gave a stiff salute, but his heart was pounding out of time. His own team? Leading men of his own?

He walked out of Jackson's office and started down the corridor. Dylan suddenly flanked him. "Okay, bro?"

"Yeah." He held out his fisted hand and Dylan brushed his knuckles against his. Sean had to get out of here. Besides needing to think on Jackson's words, he had a beautiful woman who deserved an end to what they'd started.

"Does Ben need anything else, because I'm going to jam."

"Nah, go on. She shouldn't be kept waiting." Dylan raised his chin in farewell to Sean and dropped back to speak with Chaz, who was emerging from another office.

As he sailed through the streets to reach Alisha, Sean didn't think about the spy who'd occupied the toolbox just hours before. He could only think of one thing—a certain sultry vixen.

At her place, he used the key she'd shown him hidden among a potted fern and let himself in. The place was silent, dark. His balls ached in anticipation, fueled by the adrenaline rush of the mission he'd just completed.

Fucking after a battle was a high unlike any other, and even if she had no clue what he did for a living, she could benefit from his adrenaline woody.

He pushed open the bedroom door and peeked in. His breath caught at the sight of her legs in the air and another man balls-deep in his girl.

She looked over the man's shoulder at Sean and gasped, trying to scramble into another, less raunchy position. But it was too late—Sean's emotions were already switched off.

"Oh my God, Sean!"

He only stared at her face, not giving a fuck what the other man looked like. "Guess I'm not taking you home to *Maman*." He twisted away to go.

"Wait, Sean. I didn't think you were coming back."

He kept walking, his heart a block of ice. "That's exactly the problem." He tossed her key on the coffee table on the way past and slammed the door behind him.

As he got behind the wheel of his El Camino, he realized why he'd told Ben he wasn't ready to bring her to the cabin—the connection wasn't strong enough. He had no idea what a true relationship should feel like, but having a woman eager for him to return was number one on his list.

Ben's woman Dahlia had tracked him down and hopped a flight to New York City to be with him the night before they flew out on one of the most dangerous missions Sean had ever survived. There would be plenty more like it... but who would be here to give a damn if he returned?

SUBSCRIBE to Em Petrova's newsletter for updates on this book: www.subscribepage.com/w4b4s7

Em Petrova

Em Petrova was raised by hippies in the wilds of Pennsylvania but told her parents at the age of four she wanted to be a gypsy when she grew up. She has a soft spot for babies, puppies and 90s Grunge music and believes in Bigfoot and aliens. She started writing at the age of twelve and prides herself on making her characters larger than life and her sex scenes hotter than hot.

She burst into the world of publishing in 2010 after having five beautiful bambinos and figuring they were old enough to get their own snacks while she pounds away at the keys. In her not-so-spare time, she is fur-mommy to a Labradoodle named Daisy Hasselhoff and works as editor with USA Today and New York Times bestselling authors.

Find Em Petrova at empetrova.com

Other Indie Titles by Em Petrova

Knight Ops Series
ALL KNIGHTER

HEAT OF THE KNIGHT

Wild West Series
SOMETHING ABOUT A LAWMAN
SOMETHING ABOUT A SHERIFF
SOMETHING ABOUT A BOUNTY HUNTER
SOMETHING ABOUT A MOUNTAIN MAN

Operation Cowboy Series
KICKIN' UP DUST
SPURS AND SURRENDER

The Boot Knockers Ranch Series
PUSHIN' BUTTONS
BODY LANGUAGE
REINING MEN
ROPIN' HEARTS
ROPE BURN
COWBOY NOT INCLUDED

The Boot Knockers Ranch Montana
COWBOY BY CANDLELIGHT
THE BOOT KNOCKER'S BABY
ROPIN' A ROMEO

Country Fever Series
HARD RIDIN'
LIP LOCK
UNBROKEN
SOMETHIN' DIRTY

Rope 'n Ride Series
BUCK
RYDER
RIDGE
WEST
LANE
WYNONNA

Rope 'n Ride On Series
JINGLE BOOTS
DOUBLE DIPPIN'
LICKS AND PROMISES
A COWBOY FOR CHRISTMAS
LIPSTICK 'N LEAD

The Dalton Boys
COWBOY CRAZY Hank's story
COWBOY BARGAIN Cash's story
COWBOY CRUSHIN' Witt's story

COWBOY SECRET Beck's story
COWBOY RUSH Kade's Story
COWBOY MISTLETOE a Christmas novella

Single Titles and Boxes
STRANDED AND STRADDLED
LASSO MY HEART
SINFUL HEARTS
BLOWN DOWN
FALLEN
FEVERED HEARTS
WRONG SIDE OF LOVE

Club Ties Series
LOVE TIES
HEART TIES
MARKED AS HIS
SOUL TIES
ACE'S WILD

Firehouse 5 Series
ONE FIERY NIGHT
CONTROLLED BURN
SMOLDERING HEARTS

The Quick and the Hot Series
DALLAS NIGHTS
SLICK RIDER
SPURRED ON

Also, look for traditionally published works on her website.

Printed in the USA
CPSIA information can be obtained
at www.ICGtesting.com
LVHW021635110624
782954LV00009B/556